Topsail Island Treasure

TOPSAIL ISLAND TREASURE

STEPHEN W. MEADER

Illustrated by Marbury Brown

SOUTHERN SKIES

© 1966 STEPHEN W. MEADER
© 2005 SOUTHERN SKIES LLC

All rights reserved

ISBN 978-1-931177-40-5 cloth
ISBN 978-1-931177-41-2 paperback

Library of Congress Catalog Number AC 66-10078

SOUTHERN SKIES

LITTLE ROCK, ARKANSAS

www.southernskies.com

Dedication

The republication of this book is dedicated with love to Steve Carleson---business genius, entrepreneur, trusted advisor, beloved partner, and true brother in spirit---by his best friend, Jerry Atchley.

ONE

Don Douglas didn't wait for the alarm clock to wake him. He got out of bed before six, dressed in a hurry, and went down to the kitchen, dragging his left foot on the stairs— thump, thump, thump. This was the day after Labor Day, and school would be starting tomorrow. He hoped to be well down the island before the trickle of tourists started.

Bullet, the big Chesapeake Bay retriever, thumped his tail, welcoming Don to the kitchen, and while Don was getting his orange juice out of the refrigerator, Mrs. Douglas appeared.

"Well!" she said. "Up with the birds, aren't you, son? Your father's still asleep, and goodness knows when he'll be down to breakfast."

"Last day o' vacation," Don replied between sips. "I can't afford to waste it in bed. The fall migration's started, and there ought to be a lot o' birds on the beach and the bay. I want to beat last year's count if I can."

"How many was it you saw a year ago?"

"Eighteen for sure and two more possible. If I'd had a pair o' good field glasses, I could have made certain. Anyhow, this colder weather ought to bring more flights, and I heard ducks going over in the night."

"All right." His mother laughed. "Eat a good breakfast so you won't get too hungry, and we'll look for you when we see you."

The boy finished his sausage and pancakes, drank the last of his milk, and headed for the door. The house stood only a few hundred yards from the entrance gate to Topsail Island State Park, for his father was superintendent of it. Hardly had Don reached the road when a Coast Guard jeep appeared, heading south.

"Hi!" the driver hailed. "Want a lift down-island?"

"I sure can use one," Don told him. "Are you going all the way down to the station?"

"Yep. Don't believe we've met, but I reckon you're Mr. Douglas's boy. My name's Coleman—Tom Coleman, Seaman First."

They shook hands as Don climbed in.

"What did you do—hurt your foot?" Coleman asked.

It was the question Don always dreaded, though he had grown used to it over the years.

"No," he said. "I had polio when I was six, and for a couple o' years my left leg was paralyzed. But I've learned to get around pretty well. The more I use it, the better it'll be, the doctors say. So I do a lot of hiking on the beach."

The jeep moved steadily down the straight tarred road. In the slant morning sunlight that came over the sea, the sky overhead seemed filled with flying birds. Don could see long lines of them—a thousand tiny dots that he knew were sandpipers, sanderlings, or plover. Still higher came the duck formations—V's and ragged echelons—heading across the island to the bay.

"Plenty o' birds up there," the Coast Guardsman remarked. "You seem to be interested. Know anything about 'em?"

"Not as much as I'd like. But I've watched birds a long time, and I've identified a good many different species. What I want to do is get together a list of all the kinds that come

8

to the island. When it's finished, we'll hand out copies to bird lovers that visit the island—naturalists and such."

The Coast Guard station was six miles south of the entrance gate—a little over halfway to the lower end of the beach. It had been there long before the state took over Topsail Island as a nature preserve. The lookout tower was in sight now.

"Guess you must get pretty lonely here in the wintertime," said Coleman. "You're the only boy on the island, aren't you?"

"That's right—I'm all alone," Don replied. "But I like it really because I have the feeling that nothing has changed here in hundreds of years. It's the way it was before Columbus, and that's a lot better than having the dunes all leveled off and the trees cut down, with cottages and motels everywhere."

The young seaman nodded. "I see what you mean," he said. "Well, here we are. Want to come in for a cup o' coffee?"

"Thanks, but I guess not. I'd better get on down to the beach before the tourists come."

Whistling, he went rapidly over the dune at the odd gait his friend, Bill Newton, called a "half-hitch," while the driver of the jeep looked after him with mixed pity and admiration. It was just as well Don didn't catch that look. He didn't want anybody's pity. It was hard enough to stand the fatigue and the awkwardness of being lame without having people feel sorry for him.

No sooner had he scrambled down to the loose sand below the dune than an extraordinary sight greeted him. The tide was out, and for as far as he could see, the beach was alive with birds. Quietly he sat down on a driftwood log to watch them.

Right in front of him was a mixed flock of smaller beach-runners. There were forty or fifty pale gray sanderlings, darting after each receding wave, snatching a tidbit and scurrying back before the next wave caught them. Just above them, at the edge of the wet sand, he could pick out a dozen darker birds that he recognized as semipalmated sandpipers. And with these were several tiny least sandpipers and ringed plovers. The little ringneck was a special favorite of his. It ran in quick dashes and cocked its head like a miniature robin. A gray back and white breast were set off by a smart black choker collar.

A little farther north he saw four willets, bigger than the sandpipers, with long, slim legs and necks. They were as graceful as deer, and though their color seemed an overall drab gray, the moment they spread their wings they showed a beautiful pattern of black and white markings. Two of them flew now, calling each other in soft musical whistles.

Don sat perfectly still. He had been there only a few moments when two more birds settled on the beach a dozen yards away. One was a big black-bellied plover, double the size of the ringneck, with a striking black vest. The other wore a coat of many colors—black, white, and rusty orange. It busied itself poking into empty clamshells and patches of weed, and Don grinned as he recognized an old friend—a ruddy turnstone.

As he had hoped, it looked as if this would be a big day for birds. The southward migration was in full swing, the weather was perfect for visibility, and he was early enough to be ahead of the disturbing visitors. A clamor of gulls from down the beach brought Don to his feet again, and he limped toward the noise. Proudly he thought of the improvement he had made in his ability to get over the ground. Only two years ago he couldn't have managed such an excursion, for then he was still on crutches, and the points sank deep in the loose sand.

For several hundred yards, the beach and the air above it were alive with gulls, most of them screaming loudly. A big white herring gull had picked up a clam in the surf and was soaring overhead, looking for a safe place to drop it and break the shell. The maneuver was made more difficult by a swarm of other herring gulls that swooped at their lucky brother, trying to make him let go of his prize. Finally they succeeded. His big yellow beak opened, and the clam fell, hitting the hard sand with an audible thump.

Instantly a dozen of the huge awkward birds were around it, fighting and squawking, and the original owner flew off, disgruntled, to hunt for another meal.

There were other kinds of gulls in the area, but they steered clear of the big, quarrelsome herring gulls. Don saw numbers of smaller ones—the gray-backed, black-hooded laughing gulls and the graceful ringbills, colored much like the herring gulls but with dark, narrow rings around their paler beaks.

Suddenly the squabbling mob at the edge of the surf grew silent. Some toddled awkwardly away, and others flew off over the water. The reason was soon apparent. A huge bird came sailing down to a landing. As it folded its wings and stood there in full majesty, Don held his breath. Only once before had he laid eyes on the great black-backed gull—the giant of its race—a rare visitor from far northern coasts.

The immense bird was only thirty yards away, and Don could see every inch of it. The snow-white head was held high, on a thick, proud neck. The powerful bill was a bright shade of yellow, and the legs were a pinkish gray. But it was the coal-black mantle of the back and wing coverts that made it such a striking sight. All Don could do was stand there in open-mouthed admiration.

He could have stayed to watch all morning, but time was passing, and there were miles of beach ahead. Twice he looked back to see the big bird still resting, stately and alone. Then his ears brought him a sound that promised something almost as interesting. It was the high, sweet flute-note of a piping plover. At first he couldn't find the little bird, so perfectly did its pale plumage blend with the color of the sand. Only when it ran down the beach did he see the bright black speck of its eye.

Don pulled a pencil and a small notebook from his pocket. It was time he wrote down the birds he had seen before he forgot them, and when he finished, he was surprised to find he already had a dozen on his list, all of them properly identified.

He was below the usual visitors' area now, but from where he stood, he saw two cars go by, heading south. From the assortment of casting rods tied to their roofs, he knew they were surf fishermen, bound for the rips at the lower end of the island. Many of them came during the season for channel bass or drumfish.

Don still had most of the morning ahead of him, and his leg felt strong. It was getting warm, however, and before pushing on, he took off his sneakers and socks, wrapped them in his jacket, and left the bundle under a bayberry bush on the side of the dune.

A little farther on, he could see a flock of terns flying above the incoming surf. The cool sand felt good to his bare feet, and he hurried on to have a closer look. Smaller than gulls, the terns were beautiful birds to watch, with their long slim wings and swallow-like forked tails. They flew with black-capped heads bent down, watching for small fish. Every few seconds one would fold its wings and dive like an arrow, often coming up with a two-inch minnow in its strong orange bill.

Whenever this happened, a young tern, squatting on the sand, would set up a plaintive squawking. And the cries would continue until the parent bird brought it a piece of fish. Don thought the youngsters were badly spoiled, for some were three or four months old and perfectly able to fly and fish for themselves.

As he watched, he saw that the common terns were not alone. In the flock were several much smaller birds, with shorter tails and showing a white patch in the black cap above the eyes. Their bills were gray instead of orange. He made a careful note to check them in his book of water birds, but he was almost positive they were least terns. At that moment, only a few yards from where he stood, a dark, slaty-gray bird sailed down and came to rest on the sand. In shape it was certainly another tern, but its color was vastly different. Could he be looking at a black tern? He had read that they sometimes visited the New Jersey coast, though their nesting grounds were far inland in Canada and around the Great Lakes. This one, he thought, might have stopped here before its ocean flight to the tropics.

Don was about ready to cross over to the bay shore of the island. But before he left the beach, there was one more treat in store for him. A large flock of birds that looked like dark sandpipers came soaring over, made a precision turn, and landed just above the tide. There they seemed to march in quick step, not running like the sanderlings but parading like a company of soldiers. As they turned into the sun, Don caught a glow of dusky red in their breasts and knew this was a flock of knot, called "robin snipe" by the coastal fishermen.

"Sixteen!" he whispered to himself happily. "Now, if I can do half as well over at the marsh, I'll beat my record!"

He scrambled across the low dune and the road, threaded his way through a tangle of cedar trees, and found himself facing a broad stretch of marsh and mudflats, cut by winding tidal creeks. In the foreground was a fringe of tall bulrushes. And in the distance the bay lay blue under the September sky.

This was a wholly different world from the wave-beaten sands on the seaward side of the island. Yet Don knew from experience that he would find it teeming with bird life. Slowly he made his way down through the marsh grass, his eyes on the waving plumes of the bulrushes. As he drew near, there was a sudden flapping of wings, and a dark-colored bird with a long beak flew away toward the marsh. Don jotted another name in his notebook—"green heron."

Before he could put the book back in his pocket, a harsh squawking sound came from off to his left. There, in the top of an old cedar, he saw a great mass of sticks that must have taken years to put together. It was a fish hawk's nest, and two nearly grown chicks were perched on the edge, their bills held open hungrily. At that moment one of the parent birds came in from the sea with a steady beat of powerful wings. Don saw a foot-long fish, still squirming, clutched in the claws of the older bird. The big osprey lighted in the nest, and in a few seconds the young ones were tearing greedily at their meal.

Don would have enjoyed staying to watch, but the urge to add to his list was strong. He turned back to the marsh, pushed through the high rushes, and stood looking out over the flats. It was low water, and much of the area lay drying in the sun. But in the tide creeks, big white birds were standing. He could see their long necks stretched above the marsh grass.

Cautiously he moved forward, a step at a time, trying not to alarm the waders. Already he was near enough to see that there were two kinds of white herons in the shallow creek. All of them had long spearlike beaks, but the smaller birds' beaks were dark gray. Only two or three of the tallest herons had the yellow bills that identified them as American egrets. The rest were little blue herons in their white first-year plumage.

Don watched long enough to be certain, then wrote the names in his notebook. He counted the birds he had seen and whistled under his breath. The total was up to twenty!

Then, as he stood there, still gloating over the count, there was the sound of a chugging motor on the road. He gave a grunt of disgust. Tourists—always butting in when he wanted to be alone!

TWO

Don heard the car stop right abreast of him, but out of sight beyond the strip of woods. Then a man came pushing through the trees and stopped, looking down over the marsh. He was tall and lean, with a thatch of dark curly hair, and was dressed in tan slacks and a khaki shirt. Around his neck hung a pair of field glasses.

He caught sight of the boy and waved, then started down through the bulrushes. A moment later he was there beside Don, lifting the glasses to focus on the herons.

"I see you're a bird watcher, too," he said in a low voice. "My name's Alec Cameron, from Princeton. Do you live around here?"

"Yes," Don told him. "I'm Don Douglas, and my dad's the superintendent of the park."

"Good! Perhaps you can show me some good places to see birds. Did you notice the three different species in this flock?"

"No," Don admitted. "I only spotted two—the egrets and the little blues."

"Take another look." Cameron grinned. "Over there to the left. See the one with the crest—the feathers on the back of the head? It's hardly bigger than the little blues, but there's one real difference if it's a snowy egret, as I think it is. We'll have to make them fly to be certain. Watch that bird's feet when they take off."

With Don beside him, Cameron advanced slowly toward the little creek. They had approached within a dozen yards before the herons took alarm and started upward with a great flapping of wings. The big egrets had yellow legs, Don saw, while those of all the others were darker colored. But one bird—the one he had been told to watch—had bright yellow feet on the ends of its slim black legs.

"You see?" asked Cameron. "That's the one sure way to identify a snowy—the yellow feet. What's that little book? A list of what you've seen today?"

Don nodded as he wrote down the name of the snowy egret, then handed over the book with some pride.

"Good!" said the stranger, after scanning the list. "You had a lucky morning on the beach, I see. I'd like to see the great blackback myself. Let's move along and look for some more."

They worked their way south, around a bend in the creek, and went farther out on the marsh. The tide must have started to come in, for more of the mudflats were now covered with water.

From somewhere west of them came a sound like the high-pitched barking of a dog, and Don recognized the cry at once.

"Look!" he said, pointing toward a flooded patch of marsh. "It's a black skimmer!" And sure enough, they saw a graceful bird, jet black above and white beneath, flying low over the water. Its big bright-red beak was open an inch or two, and it seemed to skim the water with its long lower "lip," leaving a ripple behind it.

Alec Cameron followed the bird with his glasses. "Here he comes back!" he exclaimed. "Probably that first run was just to stir the fish up and bring them to the top. Now he'll catch one—there—see it in his beak?"

"We have more of 'em in the spring," Don told him. "A

few nest in the dunes, and I've seen their eggs. The terns nest there, too, but the skimmers' eggs are bigger and sort of bluish with brown spots."

His companion looked at him with increased respect. "You're really interested, aren't you?" he said. "Ever thought of being a naturalist when you grow up?"

Don shied away from the question. "I haven't made any plans," he replied cautiously. "First thing I've got to do is get through high school if I can."

Cameron nodded, and his smile was understanding. "I know," he said. "You think your lameness would be a handicap. But you get around very well as it is. Does the leg give you any pain?"

"Not really. My hip gets tired if I walk too far, but I'm a lot better than I used to be. I know exercise is supposed to help, so I keep at it."

Somehow, the stranger was so direct and matter-of-fact in his questions that Don didn't mind talking about himself.

"When I was a kid," the older man remarked, "I had rheumatic fever and a bad heart. When I was your age, I didn't dare go out for athletics. But I made it through college, and I've had a pretty good life ever since."

Don thought about this as they went across the marsh. He began to feel a bond of sympathy with his new friend.

"My dad wants me to go to college," he said, "and I'd like it, too, I guess. What do you do, Mr. Cameron, besides birdwatching?"

Cameron laughed. "I teach biology at the university," he replied. "These bird trips are just a hobby, but the hiking is good for me. Best exercise there is."

Off on their left, there was a point of higher ground jutting out toward the bay. It was covered with bayberry bushes and cat briars and would be a difficult place in which to

18

walk. However, it was high enough above the flats to give them a better view.

The two were discussing whether to try it when a clear, high whistle came from a clump of bayberry. It was in two notes—"Kill-dee, kill-dee." Then a plover-like bird flew up and passed close above them.

"Did you spot his double collar?" Cameron asked. "That's a killdeer!"

Don was pleased. "It's the first one I've really seen," he said. "I've heard 'em call, of course, but generally they stay out of sight. Let me put his name down in my book. That makes twenty-three, so far!"

They scrambled up through the briars and made their way westward toward the water. On the other side of the point, there was a sheltered cove, and as soon as they were high enough to look down on it, Don pulled at his companion's sleeve.

"Ducks!" he whispered. "I can see black ducks and mallards and maybe some others."

Silently Cameron raised his field glasses and settled them on the swimming flock. "You're right," he whispered back.

"There's a pair of blue-winged teal along with the rest. Here—try the glasses."

Don took them eagerly, and after a moment spent in adjusting the focus, he found the flock of ducks in the lenses. They seemed amazingly close. The common black ducks were the most numerous, and they constantly tilted their tails in the air as they searched the bottom for food. By far the most colorful birds were the mallard drakes, with their coppery red vests and shining green heads. The blue-winged teal were obviously smaller than the others—the female a quiet little gray duck and the male handsomely marked with a white crescent in front of the eye and pale blue wing patches.

"Golly!" said Don as he handed back the glasses. "You know that makes twenty-six birds I've seen?"

Cameron chuckled. "You're not through yet," he answered. "I heard a red-winged blackbird calling, over beyond the cove. Let's go find him."

Don heard it, too—the long, clear "Ok-a-lee" of one of the commonest of coastal songsters. With the older man leading the way, they went back along the point. And just as they reached the head of the little bay, an enormous grayish bird stepped from the bulrushes a few yards away and flew off on broad wings, its dark stiltlike legs trailing behind it.

"A great blue heron!" Don exclaimed. "He must have been here all the time we were out on the point!"

"Yes," Cameron told him, "but he was pretty well camouflaged here in the reeds. I doubt if we'd have seen him if we hadn't almost bumped into him. Look—there's your redwing in that bayberry clump!"

Jubilantly Don added two more birds to his string. Twenty-eight was far more than he had hoped to find, and the day wasn't over yet.

"What do you plan to do with this list you're making?" the biologist asked.

"Well, my father likes to give the visitors little pamphlets about Topsail Island. We've already got one that tells about the trees and plants and flowers found here. I figure at least as many people are interested in birds."

Cameron nodded. "I'm sure they are. Where do you want to go next? You aren't hungry, are you? It's only about ten-thirty."

"We could try the beach again," said Don. "Or if you'd like to drive down to the inlet, we might find some different birds there."

The last idea met with the professor's approval, and in a few minutes they were rolling down the road in his little Volkswagen car. As they neared the end of the island, they could hear the roar of surf where the tide was beating in over the inlet rips. A great flock of gulls and terns filled the air above the frothy water, screaming, wheeling, and darting down after fish.

Don led the way to the edge of the bluff above the choppy waves.

"I've got all the gulls," he told his companion, "and the terns, too. But there are a couple of dark birds swimming out there. What are they—black ducks?"

Cameron studied them through the binoculars. "No!" he exclaimed after a moment. "You're in luck, Don. They're surf scoters! Take a look. See the red nob on the bill and the white patches on the head?"

Don watched them with the glasses. "Twenty-nine!" he said with satisfaction. "Gee, you've sure been a help to me. I'd never have spotted as many if I'd been alone. Do you come here often?"

"Whenever I can get away for a day. Most of the summer

I was up on the Maine coast, where a lot of the marine life is different. But I always try to visit this bit of shore during the bird migrations. Probably you don't realize it, but you're lucky to live where there's natural open space. On most of the islands, every available acre is jammed with cottages, and there are so many people on the beach, there's no room for birds to land."

"Oh, I realize it all right." Don laughed. "The school bus takes me past that kind of built-up beach every day."

"Where do you go to school?"

"Ocean Regional High, over on the mainland. It's about a forty-minute trip on the bus."

They got into the Volkswagen again and started northward. Cameron talked as he drove.

"What year are you in school?" he asked.

"Just starting sophomore year this week. I'm a little behind for my age because I couldn't go to school when my leg was still paralyzed."

"I expect you get good grades, though," said the older man. "You do plan to go on to college, don't you? If you can get into Princeton, perhaps I'll have you in some of my classes."

"I'd like that," Don replied. "But there'll be a lot of bridges to cross first. Could you stop at the house for some lunch? It must be getting close to noon."

Cameron smiled. "I'd better not, today," he said. "I doubt if your mother would want an unexpected guest. Anyhow, I must start back. I'll probably get a bite at the diner across the bridge."

Don asked him to stop when they reached the place where he had left his shoes and jacket. He recovered them, and they drove on up the island.

"Let's see," said Cameron as they came in sight of the gates at the upper end. "That should be your house, there on the left. Thanks for a good morning. It was fun having a real bird watcher for company, and I'll look you up when I come down here again."

Don was sorry to see him go. Until now, his bird studies had been his own idea, and his only help had been a good bird book. Today he felt surer of himself with an expert for a friend.

The kitchen clock said eleven-thirty when he went into the house, and his mother was just putting soup on the stove.

"You're early, Donny," she remarked. "Your father won't be home before noon. How was the morning?"

"It was great," he told her. "Maybe you won't believe it, but I got twenty-nine—more birds than I ever saw before!"

He went up to his room and started making a neat copy of the list taken from his notebook. He had no real doubt of any of his identifications, but to make doubly sure, he checked the less common birds against the pictures and descriptions in his *Water Bird Guide.*

When he heard his father's footsteps below, he hurried downstairs with the fresh copy in his hand.

"Look at this, Dad!" he called. "I bet you didn't think I could find twenty-nine different birds on the island in one morning!"

John Douglas was a big hearty man, tanned from outdoor living. "Twenty-nine?" he said. "That's a record, isn't it? This is the right time of year, of course, but you did mighty well to spot so many."

"I had a little help," Don admitted. "There was a man named Cameron down on the marsh, and he had some good field glasses."

"Alec Cameron, eh? I remember now, he checked in this morning. A professor at Princeton—nice chap. You should have asked him in for lunch."

"I did, but he didn't want to bother Mom. Does he come to Topsail often?"

"Yes. I've met him a number of times. He's a first-rate birdman, they tell me. Want to go down the island again this afternoon? I have to run down to the inlet and check on the licenses of a couple of surf fishermen."

"Sure—I'd like that. Maybe I can make it an even thirty for the day! Wouldn't that be something?"

As soon as they had finished lunch, the superintendent went to his room. In a moment, he came back with a battered old pair of binoculars in his hand.

"Here," he said with a grin. "If you're going to be a serious bird watcher, you ought to have the right equipment. They don't look like much, but they're good ones. I used 'em in the Coast Guard, back in World War II days."

"Golly!" Don exclaimed. "You mean I can keep these to use myself, whenever I want? Thanks a heap, Dad! I'll be outside. Got to see how they work!"

THREE

Even riding over the bumpy road in his father's pick-up truck, Don kept the binoculars at his eyes. Some of the leather coating had worn off, and there were dents in the exposed brass, but the lenses were still good. He found he could see shacks and gunners' blinds clear across the bay at a distance of nearly four miles. Somewhat closer, he could make out rafts of ducks resting on the water, though it was impossible to tell what species they were. As the truck neared the osprey's nest he had seen that morning, he asked his father to slow down.

"Look, Dad!" he exclaimed. "Way up above the beach—see the fish hawk coming in? There's some young ones in the nest, and she's bringing 'em what looks like a kingfish."

"How do you know it's a she?" John Douglas asked with a chuckle. "The male bird looks just the same. Say—I believe your fish hawk's in trouble!"

As Don stared upward, he saw the osprey swerve and zig-zag. Swooping down on it at bullet speed was another, even larger bird, with dark wings and a white head and neck.

"It's—it's a bald eagle!" he gasped.

The two big birds were moving too fast for a steady view through the glasses, but he could see their actions plainly enough. The eagle changed course to match its quarry, and in a split second it was almost on the other bird's back.

Stubbornly the osprey refused to drop its catch. Instead, it made a lightning-fast turn to the left, and the eagle plunged past, bringing up twenty feet below. Don couldn't hold back a cheer as the fish hawk sped toward its nest. There it dropped the still-squirming fish among the young ospreys and turned bravely to face the eagle's charge, wings back and talons spread. The bigger bird swerved aside, having no stomach for a head-on encounter. As it flapped off, Don gave a snort.

"The big coward!" he cried. "Served him right!"

"That's exactly how Ben Franklin felt." His father laughed. "He suggested the wild turkey would be a better national symbol than the bald eagle. But, anyhow, you've got another bird for your list."

Don wrote the name down promptly. Then he turned his glasses on the long stretch of beach where the tide was rising.

"Not many tourists today," he commented. "Quite a difference since yesterday."

"That's right," said his father. "Less than a dozen came through the gates today. But the holiday's just over, and there'll be other weekends later when we'll have more visitors. This is probably the best day you'll have all fall for spotting birds."

They were nearing the inlet now. "What about these fishermen you want to see?" Don asked. "Think there's something wrong with 'em?"

"Probably not. They had licenses all right when they checked in. But the State Police nailed 'em for speeding, back on the mainland, and thought they acted a bit suspicious, so they gave me a call."

There were three cars parked at the end of the road, including the jeep station wagon Don had seen passing that morning. The others were an old Chevrolet and a bigger, more powerful Cadillac. Half a dozen men could be seen in the surf or on the beach, their rod holders, bait boxes, and other paraphernalia stretched out in a line along the sand.

John Douglas strolled toward them, with Don limping in his wake. The first fisherman they came to was up on the beach, rebaiting his hook.

"Hi," the superintendent greeted him. "Nice day, isn't it? Getting any fish?"

"Only three keepers, so far," the man replied. "The ones that are biting are mostly trash—little dogfish an' sea robins."

"Well, the tide coming in may bring you better luck. Which car did you come in?"

"The jeep. Four of us came down in that. The other two guys, up yonder, were in the Chevy."

"So?" said Douglas. "What became of the men in the big car?"

"Search me. Went back in the dunes somewhere to eat their lunch, I guess. They haven't done any fishing."

John Douglas chuckled. "They didn't look like fishermen to me when we checked 'em in. Good luck, now. Maybe you'll get a striper!"

He went on along the sands, narrowed now by the rising tide, and watched some of the other men casting, waist-deep in the surf. Don, meanwhile, was scanning the beach with the glasses. A flock of laughing gulls was resting on the sand, some distance away. As he studied them, he saw a gull standing nearby that looked like a miniature edition of the others. Sharpening the focus, he realized that while it had the same black head, the wings were lighter gray and the legs a bright orange red. This, he was sure, was a different species, but he couldn't identify it till he looked in his book.

"Dad," he said, "take a look at those gulls through the binoculars. See the little one with the red legs? Do you know what it is?"

"No," his father answered after a moment. "But I can see it's smaller. We'll find out when we get home."

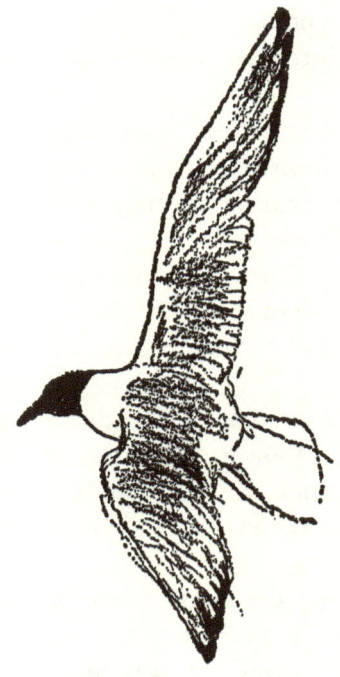

They returned to the truck and headed slowly up the island. John Douglas kept an eye on the brush-covered dunes as he drove, but if the two men from the Cadillac were picnicking there, they were well hidden.

"Oh, well," he said at length, "I guess they aren't doing anything illegal."

"What did they look like?" asked Don.

"Let's see, now. The one named Blake was a big swarthy

chap about thirty. The other one—Fallon—was smaller. Red-headed and skinny. As I said, neither of 'em looked like fishermen. They had on brand-new sport shirts in loud colors. And I didn't notice any equipment in the car—no rods or waders. Of course, they could have been in the trunk."

Don put the two men out of his mind. His father appeared satisfied that nothing further needed to be done about them, and the boy was more interested in the new birds on his list. As soon as they reached home, he rushed upstairs to get the book.

In the middle of the volume, there were many excellent color prints, and he turned to the section on gulls. After a brief search he came to the bird he had seen—a Bonaparte's gull. The dark head and pale gray wings, the small black bill and the red legs were all shown in the plate marked "adult summer plumage." Apparently it wasn't too rare on the Atlantic Coast. He had probably seen it before and mistaken it for one of the commoner laughing gulls. But, at any rate, it could be added to his list.

That evening he addressed a picture post card of Topsail Island to Professor Alec Cameron. On it he wrote: "I got 31 birds today. After you left, I saw a bald eagle and then a Bonaparte's gull on the beach. My father has given me a pair of field glasses. I hope you'll come back soon, and we can go out after more birds. But it will have to be on a Saturday or Sunday because school starts tomorrow, darn it. Yours, Don Douglas."

* * *

At seven-thirty the next morning, he was on his way. The guard at the main gate waved him through.

"Goin' to school, eh, Donny?" he called. "Kinda tough to have vacation over."

Then he was hiking across the bridge that spanned the upper inlet. Just before he reached the draw over the channel, a bell clanged, a red light flashed on, and a striped gate dropped in front of him. A big fishing boat was approaching from the landward side, her diesels idling as she waited for the bridge to open. From where he stood, Don could see the bridge tender pull his levers, and the two sections of the draw began to rise.

Everything seemed to happen in slow motion. A full minute passed before the counter-balanced roadway loomed erect against the sky. Then the boat got under way and moved leisurely toward the opening. The ebb tide was surging out between the piers, and it caught the vessel and swept her through, her tall outriggers reaching far above Don's head. At last, when she was well out in the channel, the bridge began to descend once more. The whole operation may have taken four minutes, but to the impatient boy it seemed like hours.

As soon as the gate lifted, he limped rapidly across, hailing the bridge tender as he passed his little hut. "Some day, Joe," he called, "you're going to make me late for the bus!"

"Oh, well," the man said with a laugh, "you wouldn't mind missin' a day o' school, would you?"

In a few more minutes he was off the causeway and on the next island. Half a mile away he could see the yellow school bus coming down the road, and he waited for it at the spot where it would turn around. At least twenty high-school students were already aboard.

"Hi, Don"—"Hello, Don"—called the girls and some of the boys. "Yea, Hoppy!" cried Dick Jimson. "You're lookin' fit as a flea! Goin' out for football?"

Don reddened as he took a seat. The last question had been asked with a snicker, but being called "Hoppy" was what he most resented. "Digger" Jimson was disliked by nearly everybody because of his taunting tongue. His own nickname came from the fact that his family dug clams, sold bait, and rented boats.

Bill Newton came down the aisle and swung his lanky body into the seat by Don's side. "Good to see you, Donny-o," he said with a grin. "I haven't been down to Topsail for more'n a month. What you been doing this vacation time?"

"Just hiking around the beach and the dunes, mostly. One thing I did was look for birds. Yesterday, believe it or not, I spotted thirty-one kinds!"

"Yeah? Do you think there'll be some left when the gunning season opens? I'd like to get me a few ducks."

"Shucks!" Don grinned. "What do you want to kill 'em for? You know darn well a tame duck is fatter an' tastes better. But if you're bound to shoot 'em, I guess there'll be a few around in November."

Bill laughed and changed the subject. "Didn't you do any swimming? I spent most o' my time on the beach."

"Oh, sure, I swam a lot. I can't do much in the surf, but I go in off our boat dock in the back channel. They say swimming's one o' the best kinds of exercise for someone with my trouble."

The bus crossed a long causeway and bridge over the bay, and after another mile or two, it pulled into a line of other buses unloading in front of the sprawling new high school. The youngsters got off and mingled with the chattering crowd that went in to register, pick up their schedules, and be assigned to homerooms.

Don and Bill were glad to find they would be in the same room, under a popular young science teacher named Garry Reynolds. They had heard that second-year studies were a lot harder, but for that first day, at least, they were given no homework.

Meanwhile, the football coach was prowling the corridors,

31

looking over the crop of students for likely material. He suddenly pointed a finger at the passing Bill Newton.

"You, there, with the long legs," he called. "What's your name?"

Bill told him, wondering what was coming next.

"I've seen you run," the coach said. "You're fast. Ever catch any passes?"

"Oh, sure—a few. Why?"

"Then you'd better try out for end. See you at the field at two-thirty."

Bill turned to Don in bewilderment. "Does he mean he wants me to come out for football?" he asked.

" 'Course he does!" Don told him. "You'll make it, too. Boy—what wouldn't I give for a chance like that!"

They were all excused early that first day, and Don accompanied his friend to the athletic field to watch the start of practice. No suits had been issued as yet, so the coach was content to put the boys through a series of sprints and let them line up for a game of touch football. On the third play the quarterback dropped back and let fly a long pass in Bill's general direction. The tall youngster jumped high for the ball, grabbed it, and set sail for the goal line before any opponent could get near him.

As they rode homeward in the bus, a senior who played as a regular guard on the team took the time to compliment Bill.

"It won't be that easy in a real game," he said, "but you've got the stuff if you practice hard. Hope you make it. Us islanders have to stick together. If we don't, the farmers an' landlubbers'll take over at Ocean Regional."

On the return trip, the bus let off all the other students before taking Don down to his stop at the end of the island. The driver was new on the route.

"You live down there?" he asked. "I thought Topsail Island was a game preserve or something."

"It's a state park, really," Don told him. "My dad's the superintendent. That's why I live there."

The driver must have noticed the hitch in his stride. "Don't somebody come to meet you?" he inquired. "Must be quite a walk for you."

"Shucks." Don laughed. "It's less'n half a mile. I don't mind a bit. So long, now. See you in the morning."

This time the drawbridge caused no delays, and once past the park gate, he went whistling down the road to his house. It wasn't until later, when he was eating an afternoon snack of doughnuts and milk, that an unhappy thought struck him. If Bill Newton stayed on the squad and played football, he would see a lot less of his friend this fall. Practice usually lasted till four-thirty, and a special bus carried the players home.

At least he had Bullet for company. Since there was no homework to do that afternoon, he took the dog down the path to the bay and sat on the dock, pitching blocks of wood for the retriever to fetch from the water. Bullet adored this game and would have kept it up for hours. They were interrupted by the passing of a small outboard that came down the channel.

There were two men in the boat, and though they were nearly two hundred yards from shore, Don could see their bright sport shirts plainly. He would have thought no more about them if he hadn't noticed that one was a big fellow with black hair and the other a thin little redhead.

FOUR

Don mentioned the two strangers to his father that night at supper. "Of course," he said, "there are plenty o' boats on the bay. I wouldn't have paid any attention to these two men except that they were wearing pretty wild shirts. Then I saw the big dark one and the skinny one with red hair and remembered what you told me about that pair in the Cadillac yesterday."

"Could be the same ones," his father replied. "I don't suppose you saw where they went, did you?"

"No. They stayed in the channel, and after they passed the first point, they were out o' sight."

"Oh, well, I doubt if what they're doing is any worry of ours. We don't have any authority to stop people from using the waterway. Still, it's a nice evening, and I wouldn't mind a ride in the boat. Want to come along?"

Don accepted with alacrity. He picked up his field glasses and followed his father down to the dock. The sun had barely set, and there was still plenty of daylight on the water when they took off the tarpaulin, loosed the moorings, and started the engine. The boat was a twenty-foot inboard runabout with a hundred and fifty husky horsepower. She could cruise easily at thirty-five miles an hour, but John Douglas took her down the channel at half speed.

"See anything?" he asked.

Don was sweeping the reaches of the bay with his glasses. "No small boats," he said. "There's a big bank-skiff, the kind the fishermen use, but it's over on the mainland side, just coming home, I guess. Must be five miles south of us."

His father stepped up the speed a little, following the winding channel marked by the buoys.

"Better watch the island," he told Don. "That's all I'm interested in."

A quarter of an hour later, when they were only three or four miles above the lower inlet, the boy spotted a small boat rounding a point, close inshore. It looked as if it might have made a landing on Topsail, but there was no way to be certain.

John Douglas saw it, too. "Can you make out who's in her?" he asked. "Never mind, she's headed this way, so I reckon we'll know soon enough."

He steered a little farther out into the bay and stopped the engine. "Get out a fishing rod," he told his son. "We'll drift till they pass us."

Don enjoyed this game of cops and robbers. He quickly had a line over the side and pretended to jerk the rod up and down as if he felt a bite.

"Don't overdo it," said his father dryly. "Just sit still and fish."

"Wish I had some bait on the hook," Don answered. "I've got a hunch I might catch one."

The other boat seemed to creep toward them as they waited, its outboard motor putt-putting lazily. When it was almost abreast, Don's father turned his head to look at the occupants.

"Same pair, all right," he muttered. "Now what in blazes would bring 'em here again?"

He waited till the boat was well up the bay before he

pushed the starter. Then he swung around and sent his own craft northward at full speed. They passed the two men somewhere off the home dock but didn't turn in.

"That's one o' Jimson's boats," John Douglas said. "I'd like to run up there and take a look around."

Shortly they were crossing the choppy water of the inlet and nearing the upper island. A mile or more above the bridge, a rickety dock thrust out into the bay, with four or five boats moored along its sides. The superintendent slowed down and ran close to the end of the pier.

"See that Cadillac parked up by the bait shop?" he remarked. "Put your glasses on it, Don, and read the license plate."

The car's rear was toward them, and though dusk was falling, Don found he could see the plate. "It's a New York license," he reported, and read off the numbers while his father jotted them down. Then, while the smaller craft was still a dot in the channel behind them, John Douglas turned the boat around and headed for home.

"Maybe there's nothing fishy about those two," he said, "but just to make sure, I'll ask the State Police to check up on their car."

The expedition had stirred Don's imagination, and he lay awake for some time that night, inventing reasons for the men's visits. Perhaps, he thought, they were running a moonshine still in the woods back of the dune. Or possibly they had robbed a bank and hidden the money there. But as he thought about it, he realized there was nothing to support either theory, and he finally went to sleep, as baffled as ever.

*　　*　　*

A drizzle of rain began to fall in the night, and for two days the weather alternated between overcast and stormy.

Don trudged to the bus every morning in slicker and sou'-wester, while the east wind whipped steadily across the islands. The only good thing about it, as far as he was concerned, was that football practice had to be cancelled. Bill Newton rode home with him each afternoon on the bus.

Once or twice Don discussed the odd behavior of Blake and Fallon with his friend, though they were careful to keep their voices too low for Digger Jimson to hear them. But Bill was unable to offer any fresh ideas.

For the time, at least, Don had little opportunity to add to his list of birds. The southward flights were halted by the weather, though a few gulls still haunted the beach and herons fished forlornly on the flats.

On Saturday, as the sky began to clear under a booming westerly wind, he was glad to get out on the sands again. The field glasses hung on their strap around his neck, but for the first mile or two he saw nothing on which he wanted to use them—just the familiar herring gulls and ringbills and a scattered flock of sanderlings. Then, in the distance, he saw two big dark birds wheeling and circling high in the sky. For a moment their strong flight and great wingspread made him think they were eagles. Then a third and a fourth joined them, and he realized from their numbers they must be turkey vultures—buzzards, as all the natives called them.

Through the binoculars he could make out the separate feathers at each wing tip, like five spread fingers, that distinguished their species from hawks or eagles. Then, one after another, they spiraled downward, and the dune blocked his view.

Buzzards, he knew, were carrion eaters. They must have discovered some dead animal on the road or in the woods. Hurrying now, he clambered over the dune and came out on the narrow highway. And there, a quarter of a mile to the south, he saw a huddle of black shapes in the middle of the road. Through the glasses he could see the ugly nakedness of their red necks as they fought and tugged and flapped over something on the ground.

Don went on as fast as he could, pausing occasionally for another look through the binoculars. Not till he was within a hundred yards did the first of the vultures fly away. And the last bird stayed till he was almost on top of it. Then, with an awkward scramble, it took off to join its brothers, perched in an old cedar tree.

A bloody patch was left where they had been, and in the middle of it he saw the crushed shell of a big box turtle. The poor creature must have been a female, crossing the road to lay her eggs in the sand of the beach. He supposed a Coast Guard jeep had run over her some time in the night.

His first impulse was to throw stones at the hunched watchers in the tree. Then he remembered that they were useful scavengers, intended by nature to clean up just such unfortunate messes as the dead turtle. Also they had given him another name to put down in his notebook.

On Sunday the family drove to church on the upper island, wearing their best clothes. On the way home, John Douglas slowed down as they passed the collection of shacks where the Jimsons lived. A fisherman was buying clams at the bait stand, and there were several cars parked in the sandy lot, but Don couldn't find the Cadillac among them.

"I guess our friends don't work on Sundays." The superintendent chuckled.

"What on earth is that about?" asked Mrs. Douglas in bewilderment.

"Just a private joke between Donny and me," her husband replied. "No point in trying to explain it just now."

As often happens after a fall northeaster, the month of

September settled down to being one of the pleasantest times of the year. The sun shone on the beaches with a gentle warmth, the nights were cool, and the water stayed warm enough for comfortable bathing.

Every day after he got home from school, Don took a swim in the bay. It helped him to cool off his temper after riding in the bus with Digger Jimson, for the boy from the upper island seemed bent on provoking him into a fight. His taunts about Don's lameness disgusted the other students, and once the driver threatened to put him off the bus unless he minded his tongue.

On the morning trips, there was no trouble. Digger had sense enough to keep his mouth shut when Bill Newton was present.

After supper each evening, Don worked on his school assignments. He was doing well in his classes and really enjoying some subjects. The biology lab periods under Mr. Reynolds—a friendly and understanding teacher whom Don liked more all the time—were his particular favorites. They studied the single-celled animal life of the sea and learned how great a part these tiny creatures play in furnishing food for fish, clams and oysters, crabs, and even birds. Later, Mr. Reynolds told them, they would start dissecting larger animals such as frogs. But it was the microscope and what it revealed that most fascinated Don. He began wishing he could have some kind of microscope for Christmas.

Ever since he could hold a pencil, he had been able to draw. Since he did it better than anyone else in the class, he enjoyed making sketches of what the magnifying lens showed him. As a consequence, he always got an "A" for his work.

By the beginning of October, most of the common beach birds had gone on southward, but a few flocks of sanderlings and smaller sandpipers still scurried along at the edge of the waves. One Saturday morning Don found an old crate half buried in the sand, where he could sit and watch them. He was interested in figuring out what they ate. Evidently the morsels they found were of fairly good size and quite plentiful.

At first he thought they must be picking tiny minnows out of the water. But when he went down into the shallow ripples, no fish of any kind could be seen. Then, out of the corner of his eye, he spotted half a dozen little gray creatures, smaller than his fingernail, rolling down the sand in the wash of a wave. When he sprang forward to catch one, they suddenly disappeared as if by magic.

Don squatted on his heels and waited, perfectly still, for the next wave to come up. He was fairly sure now that the little animals weren't washed in by the tide, but where did they hide themselves between waves?

As the advancing ripple swept past his feet, he saw something move in the sand right in front of him. Two furry feelers emerged, then a head with eyes, then the whole body of a tiny egg-shaped crab. Don tensed himself and shot out his hand, seizing the squirming mite before it could burrow into the sand.

He examined every part of the little creature closely but still had trouble figuring how it could vanish so quickly. The only clue was a pair of appendages at the tail that looked like miniature back-hoes.

Don waited for the next wave, put the little crab down in half an inch of water, and watched intently. Its movement was lightning fast. Less than a second passed before it had dug into the sand, rear end first, and was completely buried. The amazing thing, he thought, was that the sandpipers ever caught them at all.

There were other living things on the beach, he knew. For years he had been familiar with the little fiddler crabs, whose burrows were up in the dry sand above the tide. They averaged an inch to three inches across when their legs were spread out, but they were so nearly the color of the sand that one rarely saw them except after a long, motionless wait. Then the black eyes on stalks would appear suddenly at the mouth of a hole. If nothing moved nearby, the head of the crab would follow, then the body. It would dash nervously a few feet to explore an empty shell in search of food. And at the first hint of danger, it would retreat with incredible speed to its burrow.

Other creatures he sometimes saw were the tiny beach fleas, or sand hoppers. They were animals rather than insects, and he knew that, like the ghost crabs, they lived on waste matter, cleaning up old fish heads, clam and crab shells, and keeping the beach tidy. It was next to impossible to catch one, for they jumped too far and too fast.

That afternoon Don's father took him to the high-school football game, and he cheered for the Ocean team. The biggest excitement came for him when Bill Newton, sent in as a substitute right end in the last quarter, caught a long pass and outfooted the safety man for the touchdown that won the game.

Don had no chance to talk to Bill that afternoon, but on Monday morning as they rode the bus, he congratulated his friend.

Bill laughed it off as usual. "That was luck," he said. "When our regular end got hurt, the other team quit worrying about passes. So nobody bothered to cover me on that play. Next time, I guess they'll be laying for me."

That night the temperature dropped into the low thirties by bedtime, and John Douglas predicted there would be frost in the morning. Don went to bed with his window open but pulled up a down quilt over the blankets. As he snuggled there in comfort, a sound came to his ears—a distant clamor like the yelping of a pack of hounds. He knew what it was. The geese were flying southward through the night. With his eyes closed, he could picture them thousands of feet above the dark coast, their strong wings beating steadily as they flew in a great, ragged V behind the wise old gander who led them. Now he could believe that fall had really come.

When he woke the next morning, there was white rime on the lawn, and his mother's flowers hung wilted on their stalks. He put on a sweater under his windbreaker for the trip to school and felt none too warm as he tramped across the inlet bridge.

His friend, the bridge tender, gave him a hail. "Reckon you heard the geese flyin'," the man remarked. "Goin' to have an early winter."

As the day advanced, however, a bright sun raised the temperature, and by Thursday of that week the air was like summer again. The football team would be playing away from home, so Don promised himself a whole Saturday of beachcombing and bird spotting. Unfortunately that night the barometer took a sharp drop, and the radio weatherman forecast a southerly storm. It began blowing strongly up the coast on Friday. Before Don got home from school, the rain was descending in sheets and the wind howling at forty miles an hour. Drenched and buffeted, he struggled up the back steps and into the kitchen.

"If this keeps up," he told his father at suppertime, "I'll have to spend the whole weekend in the house!"

The superintendent laughed at him. "Don't you know," he said, "that when a storm comes from the south, it blows itself out in a day or less? My guess would be you'll wake up to sunshine tomorrow."

Don didn't argue, for he knew his father had lived on the coast all his life. He got his homework out of the way that evening and went to bed to the sound of wind and rain still lashing the house. In the morning he woke early. And sure enough, a beam of bright sun was shining in his face!

FIVE

Half an hour after breakfast, Don was well down the island. There might be people around later, and he wanted to visit some of his favorite spots before they came.

Instead of following the beach, he hiked along behind the dunes, skirting the marsh and the bay. With the glasses he had already picked out small flocks of ducks in some of the tide creeks. Now, quite close to him, he saw a pair that were either redheads or canvasbacks. From the very pale gray of the back feathers, he thought they must be canvasbacks, though he had heard that the species was rare along the Jersey coast. The head and neck of the drake were a deep red-brown, and as it turned to swim toward shore, Don saw its black breast. The female's back was a shade darker gray, and her neck was buff-colored.

He let the glasses dangle on their strap and got out his notebook to jot down a description of the ducks. But before he had time to write a word, something moved in the reeds, only a few yards from where he stood. Don stayed motionless and watched. After a moment, a bird stepped daintily out into an opening between the stems. It was much like a willet in coloring, but taller and with a slenderer neck. Its long bill curved downward, too, quite differently from that of the willet.

Don thought he remembered seeing pictures of such a

wading bird. The name "curlew" popped into his mind, but he couldn't be sure without checking the bird book. At any rate, he had two new ones to add to his list.

Hearing the honking in the night had made him expect to find geese, and he was disappointed that so far none had appeared. Then he recalled that the big Canadian geese were grain-eaters, and if any had landed in the bay, they would now be in some cornfield on the mainland. Their habit was to come back to the water to spend the night, and the best time to see them was just after daybreak before they took off.

As if to prove him wrong, he sighted a flock of big birds in a cove a few minutes later. They were tipping their tails up and feeding on something there in the shallow water. Don focused his binoculars on them. When he got a good view of one that wasn't diving, he realized that they were brant—smaller cousins of the Canadians. They must have found a patch of eelgrass, which he knew was their favorite food.

After watching them for a while, he cut back through the woods to the road and started walking south again. There was the sound of a car approaching from behind him, and he stepped off on the shoulder. Just as he turned to look, a horn tooted, and a little green Volkswagen came to a stop.

"Ahoy, Don!" called Alec Cameron. "Looking for a ride?"

Don greeted his friend with a grin of pleasure and climbed in beside him. "I was sort of hoping you'd come down today," he said. "See these glasses Dad gave me? I've spotted some new birds since you were here."

He proceeded to tell the older man about the gray wading bird he had seen and described it carefully.

"It was a curlew, all right," Cameron replied. "The down-curved bill settles that. I'd say it was a Hudsonian curlew, sometimes called a whimbrel. They're fairly common around here, but so shy they aren't often seen."

"Then," Don went on, "I saw a pair of canvasback ducks, and there's a flock of brant geese back there in a cove. I'm pretty sure I heard some big honkers last night, but they've probably gone to the mainland to feed."

"Right. I passed a cornfield where there were at least a dozen Canadas—likely part of the same flock you heard."

He slowed the car and pointed off to the right. "Look," he said. "See that big brown hawk coming in over the flats? If you don't have a marsh hawk on your list, you've got one now. That's the female—the male bird is gray. See the long tail? It's quite a bit longer than most other hawks', and another way to identify the marsh hawk is that it flies low most of the time, so it can watch for frogs."

Don put down the glasses and wrote busily in his notebook. "Gee!" he exclaimed. "You know that makes thirty-six? Thanks a lot, Mr. Cameron!"

"Call me Alec, Don. We're old friends now. How's school going?"

"O.K., I guess. I like biology best."

"Good for you! That's my subject, so I'm specially pleased. Anything else been happening?"

Don hesitated. He didn't like to talk about Blake and Fallon until he knew more about what they had been doing on the island.

"Let's see," he said. "I did find some little tiny crabs in the edge of the waves. They dug into the sand so fast that I was lucky to catch one. He was only about this big," he explained, holding his fingers less than a quarter of an inch apart, "and he was the shape of an egg."

Cameron nodded. "A mole crab," he said, "sometimes called a Hippa crab. They burrow faster than any other

46

animal I've ever seen. Did you notice the little shovels on his tail?"

"Yes, I saw 'em. There must have been thousands along there in the ripples. Are they what the sandpipers eat?"

"Mole crabs and baby shrimp and even smaller animals called copepods. There's really plenty to feed on along the edge of the tide."

The professor's sharp eyes had spied something flying over the bay, and he stopped the car once more. "Come on," he told Don, "let's cut over toward the marsh. I think some ducks just settled on the water."

They hurried westward down the slope and entered the fringing bulrushes on the edge of a little tidal creek.

"Easy, now," Cameron whispered. "I think they're close."

He led the way quietly for another few paces, then thrust his binoculars out between the stalks. Coming up beside him, Don did the same. At once he saw a small flock of ducks gathered there on the still water.

"We're lucky," the biologist breathed. "It's a mixed flock —some blacks and mallards, but there are several others. Look—see the drake with the long, spiky tail feathers? That's a pintail. And just beyond him is a pair of widgeon. The male's head and neck are a reddish buff. Then, over to the left, do you see the ducks with big square-shaped bills? The drake's green head looks almost like a mallard's. Those are shovelers."

Don was following where he pointed with his own glasses, and he spotted all three species without difficulty. All the males of the different types were handsome, but each had his own special coloration. The females were harder to tell apart, for nearly all were a demure grayish brown.

"That's a pretty rare sight," said Cameron. "I've often seen pintails and mallards together, and there are almost always a few black ducks. But finding shovelers and widgeon in the same flock is pure luck."

"Gee!" Don crowed. "That gives me thirty-nine birds! Last time I saw you I was hoping to make it thirty. Do you suppose I can ever get it up to fifty?"

The older man laughed. "I wouldn't put it past you. After all, you'll have the spring migration ahead of you, and that will bring a different group, more beach birds and waders. But you're not through yet this fall. By getting here at sundown or very early in the morning, you can probably see some Canada geese. They raft in the coves at night. Then there's just a chance you might spot another duck or two—a little bufflehead or a golden-eye. I doubt if you'll see any more herons. The bittern, for instance, is hard to find, and so's the night heron."

Don had seen a movement far out on the bay and was busily focusing his glasses. "Look!" he cried. "There's some kind of big bird diving, out there across the channel. He just came up again. Doesn't look exactly like a duck—his bill's too sharp. See him? He has a black head and neck and a gray back."

"I've got him now," Cameron answered after a moment. "It's a loon, Don—a great northern diver! Except when they're migrating, they're usually seen in fresh water lakes up north. But there's your fortieth bird, already!"

"What's he diving for out there in deep water?" the boy asked.

"The loon's a fish-eater," said the professor. "He can swim like an arrow, and when a school of fish passes below him, he goes after them—usually gets one, too."

They watched the ducks for a while, then started back to the car.

"I doubt if I'll see you again until around Thanksgiving,"

said Cameron. "This has been a pretty good morning, though, and I wish you luck in finding more birds to add to your census. Want to ride back with me? This time perhaps I'll take you up on that offer of lunch if it's still open."

There were only a few visitors to the island that day. On the drive north Don saw little groups of them along the beach, staring off over the sea, unhappy because the water was too cold for swimming. For the rest of the fall and winter, Topsail would be a deserted place.

"Don't you get pretty lonely down here in cold weather?" Alec Cameron asked.

"Not me! I like it as long as I can get out on the dunes and the beach. There's always something to see. After a big storm, for instance. The ocean washes up a lot of queer stuff."

"That sounds interesting. I must remember to come for a visit after the next northeaster hits."

They parked in the dooryard, and Don led his friend into the kitchen where Mrs. Douglas greeted him with pleasure.

"You won't mind if I give you a simple lunch?" she said. "It's what we have every Saturday—hot soup and sandwiches with apple pie for dessert."

"That'll be wonderful," the professor told her, and soon they were seated at the kitchen table. They talked of many things. Cameron described some of his work at Princeton and the trips he took to study animal life in such distant places as Labrador and the Caribbean.

"You know, Don," he said, "those little sanderlings you see running on the beach were all born far up in the Arctic. That's their nesting ground. In the spring, the flocks try to arrive in northern Labrador about the time the snow melts. The baby chicks run the risk of being killed by owls and foxes and weasels. But their parents protect them as well as they can and teach them how to hide on the tundra, where their gray and brown feathers blend with the vegetation. By August they're big enough to fly, and the southward migration starts.

"It may take weeks to reach these beaches, but here in the warmer water they find plenty of food to strengthen them for the rest of the long journey. Down the coast they move, stopping to feed occasionally, but always flying south. From Florida some cross to South America, and a few sanderlings have been known to migrate all the way to Patagonia, at the southern tip of the South American continent."

"Gosh!" Don exclaimed. "That must be a lot of distance to cover!"

"It is. By the coastal route they travel, it's more than eight thousand miles from Labrador to Cape Horn. But by the next February, they're heading north again."

"How do the scientists know it's the same sanderlings that travel so far?" asked Don.

"By banding them—catching a few birds and putting a tiny band on one leg. Then other men, down in the Argentine, find a banded bird and report back to us."

"It must be a fascinating thing to study," Mrs. Douglas put in. "Donny, doesn't it make you want to be a biologist or whatever a bird scientist is called?"

"An ornithologist," Cameron answered. "I'm not one really—just an amateur bird watcher. But you're right, Mrs. Douglas. It makes a good life for a man."

He left soon after lunch, and Don spent the afternoon revising his bird list and checking each new find against the book. He was hoping to spot still another bird before the day ended. When his father came home at five o'clock, Don asked if he would drive him down the island after supper.

"I've got my record up to forty birds, now," he explained. "But I bet we'd see some Canada geese coming in if we're there around sunset."

John Douglas was willing to take the ride, and shortly after six they were on the road. The sun had barely set behind the mainland woods when they passed the Coast Guard station. The western sky was full of orange and violet tints. From his right-hand seat, Don was scanning the heavens, watching and listening for geese.

"Hold it, Dad," he said. "Let's turn off the engine for a minute. I thought I heard something."

As they coasted to a stop, the sound reached them—a faint, hoarse honking that grew more distinct moment by moment. Then, more than a mile away above the bay, Don saw the huge V approaching. It was made up of hundreds of tiny black dots, any one of which would have been invisible alone.

"Heading right toward us," Don's father exclaimed. "Where do you think they'll light?"

"There's a cove right over there. It's pretty well sheltered by a strip of marsh. Let's leave the car here and go down."

They were hidden by the cedars before the geese came near enough to be frightened off. From their cover, they heard the honking loud overhead as the flock circled, reconnoitering the bay. Then the big birds settled on the water with a series of splashes.

"Come on!" Don urged. "Right down there we can see 'em through the reeds!"

His father was close behind him as they pushed cautiously in among the bulrush stems. Then they both stood frozen at the sight spread before them. The huge gray birds, with their black necks and white collar bands, sat preening themselves on the rippled surface of the cove, so near that no field glasses were necessary. There must have been three or four hundred of them.

Occasionally one would utter a small, contented sound, quite different from the flight call. Then others would reply till the whole secluded bay was full of their gentle gabbling.

"Yes, sir, son," John Douglas whispered. "I'm mighty glad I came!"

They stayed a few more minutes, then crept back to the dune, careful not to alarm the rafted geese. As they rode homeward, the deep satisfaction in Don's heart came from something more than adding another bird name to his list. He had seen a sight he knew he would never forget.

SIX

The season for hurricanes was over, or so Don's father assured him as October passed. There had been the usual number of tropical storms reported during the early fall, but each one had exhausted its fury on the Gulf Coast or had whirled out to sea without damage to the New Jersey beaches.

Nevertheless, one evening in the first week of November, the radio began broadcasting gale warnings. A big hurricane, this time called "Ida," had passed the Bahamas and was heading for Cape Hatteras. At its present pace, the announcer said, the storm would be off the Delaware capes in another twenty-four hours.

With that much time to get ready for a blow, the shore people went methodically about their preparations. Store windows in the deserted resort areas were boarded over, and neon signs were taken down. The few boats left in the water were quickly hauled ashore. And housewives laid in supplies of food, in case the weather made shopping impossible.

School let out early the next day. Already the wind was coming out of the east in fifty-mile-an-hour gusts, and the sky was leaden gray, ridged with dark scudding clouds. When Don got off the bus, he had to brace himself against the blast. It was a struggle to cross the long bridge, and several times he was glad to rest, clinging to the guard rail. When he reached the tender's shack, the man on duty beckoned him inside.

"Looks like a big one." Don panted as he sipped coffee gratefully.

"Could be." The bridge tender nodded. "One good thing, though—no fishin' boats are out. Last one come in half an hour ago."

A radio on the shelf beside the telephone was playing rock 'n' roll music as they talked. Now it broke off, and a man's voice came crackling on the air.

"Here's the latest hurricane bulletin," he said. "The center has now reached a point a hundred and fifty miles off Ocean City, Maryland. Wind velocity on shore, sixty-eight miles per hour. Estimated velocity near the center, nearly one hundred and fifty. However, the course of the storm appears to be turning more to the eastward, and it is possible the full force of the gale will miss the New Jersey coast. Storm tides are probable, and wind velocities will be high."

"Hm," said the bridge tender, "I bet that's good news in Atlantic City. They git the jitters any time there's a real blow."

Don thanked him for the coffee and lurched out into the wind again. At home he found his mother watching anxiously by the window.

"I was worried they wouldn't let you come home till the regular time," she said. "I expected the rain to start any minute, and if you'd been out in it, you'd be soaked."

"All safe and sound." He laughed. "Besides, didn't you hear the storm's moving off to sea?"

At that moment there came a wilder rush of wind, and rain rattled like shot against the eastern windows.

"Gee, Mom!" said Don. "I guess I *was* lucky to get home when I did."

He went up to his room to study his bird guide. He knew most of the pictures and descriptions by heart, but if an unusual species should come his way, he wanted to be ready to identify it. After all, he needed only nine more birds to make an even fifty!

It was still raining and blowing when he closed the book and turned to his home work. The dark shut down early, but inside the house the family was dry and snug. After a little, the Chesapeake came nuzzling at Don's hand, asking to be let out.

"You crazy or something?" he said to the dog. "All right, but I bet you won't like it. Wait till I get a slicker on."

They went out by the back door, which was sheltered from the wind. As soon as he rounded the corner of the house, a gust caught at Don's slicker and nearly ripped it off of him. It was all he could do to keep his feet by leaning into the gale. Then Bullet came toward him, holding some bulky object in his mouth.

"Come back in the lee o' the house," Don shouted. "Let's see what you've found."

By the light from the kitchen window, he looked at the thing the dog was carrying. It was a big bird, he realized with a shock. A great dark wing trailed on the ground, and he could see a long, straight yellowish beak with a hawklike hook at the tip.

"Here," he told Bullet, "let me have it. Good dog!"

The bird weighed less than he expected, but under the wet feathers it was still warm. He wondered whether it was dead or merely stunned. Once inside, he spread it on the kitchen table, marveling at the wingspread.

"Dad," he called, "can you come here a minute?"

His mother was the one who answered. "What is it, Donny? Do you need anything?"

"No, Mom," he replied hastily. "Just something I wanted to show Dad."

Soon his father came lounging out. "Whew!" he whistled under his breath. "You're right, son. Mother'd have a fit if she saw that thing on her table. What kind of bird is it?"

"I'm not sure, but I think it's a shearwater. They're ocean birds and never come ashore unless they're blown in by a storm. I reckon he flew against the house and Bullet heard the bump."

John Douglas laid a hand on the bird's breast. "Feels like a heartbeat," he whispered, "but I can't be certain. Leave him there a bit and see if the warmth revives him.

"I was going to ask you to watch him while I run upstairs for my book," said Don, and when his father agreed, he sped away. In thirty seconds he was back.

"Look," he panted. "Here's the picture. I bet it's a cin— cinnereous shearwater! See the brown color on the head and back—and the yellow bill? You can tell a shearwater by that hook at the tip of the beak and the tiny legs. I doubt if he could even stand up on land."

As he spoke, the bird moved a trifle, and its eye opened.

"O.K., Buddy," Don murmured. "Don't get scared. I'll put you outside in a minute, when I'm sure you're all right."

He lifted one of the long dark wings to see if it was broken and disclosed the underside, which was white like the breast. Nothing seemed wrong with either wing.

"What a flyer he must be!" said Don's father. "Look at that wingspread! It's nearly four feet from tip to tip."

At that moment the shearwater shook itself and began to struggle.

"We'd better get him out o' here," said Don. "Give me a hand, Dad."

Together they carried the bird outside, away from the house, and tossed it into the air. And immediately it was flying seaward with strong wingbeats, right into the teeth of the gale.

Before he went to bed, Don wrote a note to his friend Alec Cameron. He described the bird in detail, drew a sketch of the beak, and asked the scientist's opinion. "I'd call it a cinereous shearwater," he wrote. "I looked up 'cinereous' in the dictionary, and it means 'ash-colored.' This one looked more brown than gray, but then, he was pretty wet. You said you'd like to see the beach after a hurricane, and this is as close to one as we'll probably get this year. Why don't you come down this Saturday?"

By morning the wind and rain were over. The air had that crystal-blue clarity that sometimes comes after a storm, and Don felt glad to be alive as he crossed the bridge to catch the school bus.

In history class that day, they were discussing old buccaneering days in the Caribbean.

"With Spain, France, and England all more or less at war with each other," said Miss Carter, the teacher, "fortunes could be made by capturing enemy ships. It was just a short step from that to outright piracy. Some historians say that during the seventeenth and eighteenth centuries as many as a thousand pirate vessels were at work on the Spanish Main and along the Atlantic Coast of America. Often their captains were in league with colonial governors and other officials, who grew rich on the proceeds. So the pirates could sail boldly into some of our ports, and nobody laid a hand on them."

She paused and looked around the room. "I'm sure you

boys are interested in pirates. Can you name any famous ones?"

Hands were up in an instant. "Blackbeard," said one boy. "Cap'n Henry Morgan," another put in. But most of them thought first of Captain Kidd.

"Kidd was right around here!" said Dick Jimson. "Folks say he buried a lot o' treasure on Topsail Island."

"What's your opinion, Don?" Miss Carter asked. "You live there."

Don shook his head and grinned. "If Kidd's treasure's on Topsail," he replied, "I never found it. No, ma'am, I reckon that tale's just made up."

Digger Jimson glared at him angrily. "Why," he cried, "we've rented boats to men that were huntin' for it!"

"That will do, Richard!" Miss Carter rebuked him. "To anyone who knows the facts, buried treasure here seems unlikely. Can anyone tell me what happened to Captain William Kidd?"

Nobody could, so she gave them the story. "He was tried for piracy in England and hanged on Execution Dock in 1701. At the time, he swore there was no treasure, but some sixty thousand dollars' worth was found hidden on his ship and on Gardiner's Island, off Long Island. It seems likely that that was all he had saved from his piratical ventures.

"Now—what can anyone tell us about Blackbeard?"

"His name was Edward Teach," Bill Newton surprised them by answering. "He was buddy-buddy with the king's governor in North Carolina, but after some o' the murders he committed, the folks in Virginia got fed up with him. A Virginia ship caught him in Ocracoke Inlet, an' he was finally killed. I know about it because my dad's been down that way."

"Very good, Bill," said Miss Carter. "Thank you. Now, it's

58

probably true that some wrecked Spanish galleons in the Caribbean still have gold and silver aboard, but I doubt very much if any of it got as far north as the Jersey shore."

"Aw, what does she know about it?" Jimson grumbled under his breath. "'Course there's treasure buried 'round here, an' I aim to find it!"

The boys who had heard him swarmed around him at noon recess, full of curiosity.

"Come on, Digger—tell us why you're so sure!" they begged. "You want some help findin' it? Where is this treasure, anyhow?"

But he shut up like a clam. "Shucks!" he told them. "You think I want the whole county messin' into my business? I just know, that's all. An' when the time comes, I'll prove it."

Don was somewhat disturbed. Jimson had mentioned renting boats to treasure hunters, and immediately his thoughts jumped to Blake and Fallon. Could that have been what they were doing on Topsail Island?

*   *   *

Saturday came at last, and the sun was still shining. Up early, Don posted himself in the front yard, watching the entrance gate near the bridge. Two or three cars full of visitors were checked through, but none of them looked familiar. At last he saw the little green Volkswagen coming down the road.

"Hi, Don!" called Cameron. "All set? Let's go!"

As they drove down the island, he asked Don about the storm.

"It didn't do much real damage," the boy answered. "Dad says there's some erosion farther down—the shape o' the beach is changed, and waves washed over the dunes in a few places. They've got most o' the sand cleared away, though."

Below the Coast Guard station, they came to a place where a small bulldozer was being used to remove a two-foot drift of sand from the roadway.

"Looks as if nobody's been south of here," Cameron remarked. "Let's leave the car and go on afoot."

The beach below had a wild, battered look that Don knew from other storms. Gullies had been washed in the usually level sand, and up along the foot of the dunes there were jumbled heaps of driftwood, shells, and seaweed. Streamers of weed even hung from the lower limbs of cedar trees, showing how high the waves had been flung.

"Let's see what the sea's brought in," said the professor, poking among the flotsam. "Plenty of whelk shells, and here's a live whelk. See how he's pulled the lid down on his door?"

Don had picked up several of the empty shells, looking for a perfect one. At last he found it—a huge white spiral with a lining of lovely orange. He knew his mother would like it for the mantel in the living room. The beach was strewn with whelks' egg cases—strange, ropelike things, made up of buff-colored disks. They were about two feet long and looked like Hawaiian *leis*. Each little section held a lot of eggs—or had at one time. There were also the flat, almost rectangular skate egg cases, dark and leathery, about three inches long and an inch and a half wide. At each of the four corners was a little spine, bent like a hook. They came from a flat brownish-colored fish with a long ratty tail.

"The old-time beachcombers called them mermaids' purses," said Cameron, picking up one of the odd-looking things. Don had not known that name before, and he handled it with more interest. Then he put it in his pocket to take home for his collection. "Mermaid's purse" was a pretty name for it, he thought.

A little way off, as they moved down the beach, he caught sight of a big horseshoe crab with a dark brown shell as large as an inverted washbowl. As they started toward it, Cameron chuckled.

"It may surprise you to know this," he said, "but Mr. Horseshoe, there, is one of the oldest animals on earth. Millions of years before the dinosaurs that fellow lived in the ocean—just exactly the way you see him now. Practically all other living things have changed their forms or died out through the ages. But the horseshoe crab stays on."

Don went up to the creature and touched it cautiously with his foot. But the shell gave off an empty, hollow sound, and when he kicked it harder, it tipped over. There in the wet sand where the shell had lain, he saw something that glinted like metal.

"Hey!" he cried. "Somebody dropped his money! A half dollar, it looks like."

The coin was partially buried, but he picked it up and brushed away the grains of sand. It was bigger than a half dollar, and the edges were worn and uneven, but it was silver beyond any doubt.

"Let me have a look," said Cameron. And he pulled out a little pocket microscope to examine it more closely.

"Well!" he exclaimed. "Do you know what you've found? It's a very old Spanish dollar. You've read about 'pieces of eight' in books like *Treasure Island*, I expect. That's what this is—a real piece of eight, probably minted in the late 1600's. See the king's head? It looks to me like Carlos II, who reigned from about 1665 on."

"What's it worth?" asked Don practically. "A dollar?"

Alec Cameron laughed. "If it's a genuine piece of eight, as I have every reason to believe, you might get anywhere from twenty-five dollars up!"

SEVEN

Don stood there with his mouth hanging open. "A Spanish piece of eight!" he repeated. "But where'd it come from? Do you think there's buried treasure here and it was washed out by the storm?"

"That's possible, I suppose," Cameron replied. "But I doubt it. You see these Spanish dollars were used in trade all along the coast. They were called pieces of eight because storekeepers often cut them into eight pieces to make smaller change. That's where we get the expression 'two bits,' meaning a quarter, or 'four bits' for half a dollar.

"So you see it could have been dropped by almost any sailor or fisherman. The sand would have covered it quickly, and it may have been here under the beach for a hundred years or more, until the storm turned it up."

They went on southward, looking for any other odd things that might have been left by the waves. But Don's thoughts weren't on the search. When Alec Cameron found an old wooden belaying pin, he commented politely but paid little attention to the object.

The professor looked at him quizzically. "What's on your mind, boy?" he asked. "Anything troubling you?"

Don confessed then. He told of what had happened that week in history class. "I can't help thinking," he said, "that maybe Digger Jimson knows something more than he'll tell about pirate treasure. It would sure be a headache for my father if the word got around that Captain Kidd or somebody had buried a lot of gold on Topsail Island. Think of the mobs we'd get down here!"

Cameron nodded thoughtfully. "Yes," he said, "I can understand what worries you. But there's no need to tell anyone about the coin you found. Just put it in a safe place and forget it for a while."

"I guess you're right," Don had to agree. "If there's no more talk about it, maybe the fuss'll die down."

They had gone nearly a mile along the beach before they thought of turning back. Then, just as Cameron was suggesting that perhaps they had come far enough, Don spied something in a hollow at the base of the dune.

"Hey!" he exclaimed. "What's that over there? It looks like a girl's head in the sand!"

They hurried to the spot, and the scientist began to chuckle. "You're right," he said. "It's a girl's head—a figurehead off a ship! Give me a hand with her."

Together they dug away the sand with their fingers. The wooden figurehead was chipped and cracked, and all the gilt paint had worn off, but they could see it must have been a fine bit of carving when it was new. The features were regular, and the sculptured hair curled back handsomely from the smooth brow. But with all their digging, they were still unable to lift the statue from its resting place. That, they found, was because it was attached to a huge piece of wood—the bow timber of a wrecked ship.

"Need a shovel for that," Don panted. "I don't suppose you've got one in your car?"

"No, but I'm pretty sure they'd have one up at the Coast Guard station. Why don't you stay here with the lady, Don? I'll trot up there and bring some tools."

Don realized that the scientist could probably make better time alone, and he contented himself with sitting down to study the figurehead. First of all, he began scraping away the crust of sand and salt. The wooden carving was joined to the ship's stem just below the lady's breast. She seemed to be growing out of the vessel itself and straining forward as if to watch the breaking seas ahead.

With a clamshell, Don carefully cleaned the bust to a point an inch or two above the ship's timber. And there, barely visible, he came on letters, cut into the wood. As nearly as he could make out, they were the initials of the carver. He tried to follow their outline with his fingernail. The first was certainly an "E" and the second either a "K" or an "R." After them came two figures that looked like an "8" and a "5."

Don was still speculating on what they meant when he heard the chugging of engines on the road just above him. Standing up, he saw both the Volkswagen and a jeep truck with the Coast Guard insignia on its side.

"Hi!" he called. "I've found something more!"

In a moment Cameron joined him, along with young Tom Coleman, the seaman who had once given Don a lift. Each of them carried a shovel.

"Well, Buddy"—the Coast Guardsman greeted him with a grin—"I hear you want to help out a lady in distress!"

"Here she is," Don told him. "And say, Alec, while you were gone, I scraped off the sand. Look at what I found."

Cameron knelt and examined the letters with his pocket microscope. "Looks like 'E. K. 85,'" he said. "The figures probably give us the date of the ship's launching."

"Let's dig the whole thing out," Coleman put in. "Maybe we can find out the name o' the ship."

He set to work with a will, while the professor dug from

the other side. In fifteen minutes, they had gone down half a dozen feet into the sand, but the great bow timber still stood solid as a rock.

"You don't suppose," Coleman panted, "the whole wreck is here under the dune?"

Cameron mopped his forehead with a handkerchief. "Hard to believe," he said, "but I suppose it's possible."

"I'm worn out shoveling," the seaman groaned. "Let me try another trick—with the jeep."

He scrambled up to the road and was back in a moment, driving the tough little truck down into the sand. On the rear of the four-wheel-drive vehicle was a winch, and from it Coleman pulled out a length of stout wire rope. With Cameron's help he looped it around the base of the ship's timber and made it fast with the hook fastened to the end. Then he got in behind the wheel.

"All right," he called, "stand clear!"

The engine came to life with a roar, and as he let in the clutch, the wheels began to churn up sand. In a moment the truck was axle-deep, but it had made no forward progress.

Coleman put the jeep in neutral with the motor running. Then he set the hand brake and pulled another lever that started the winch.

"This ought to do it!" he shouted above the engine noise. But all that happened was that the truck pulled itself backward, out of the grip of the sand.

When he had released the winch and turned off the ignition, the Coast Guardsman got out. He stood there with a comical expression of frustration on his face.

"I give up!" he said mournfully. "That thing must go all the way down to China!"

"I imagine you were right before," Cameron told him. "The whole keel of the vessel is buried here under the dune,

and the stem is solidly mortised into it. If we want to salvage the figurehead, we'll have to cut it loose."

Don agreed with him. "My dad's got a good chain saw," he said. "Why don't we go and get that?"

"Good idea," the professor replied with a nod. "And, Tom, there's something you might do if you'd like. Tell your commander at the station what we've found and ask him to look up all the wrecks along this shore since 1885. Maybe we can find out the name of the ship and the port she sailed from."

Coleman was enthusiastic. He boarded the jeep, Cameron and Don got into the Volkswagen, and in two minutes both vehicles were headed up the island.

*　　*　　*

At four o'clock that afternoon there were five people gathered in the Douglases' living room. Alec Cameron was there, and Lieutenant Mason from the Coast Guard, as well as the three members of the superintendent's family. In the center of the room stood the massive oak bow timber with its forward-reaching figurehead. They had sawed it off some three feet below the carving, and a thorough sudsing with soap and water had made it clean enough to occupy a place of honor on Mrs. Douglas's best rug.

"I think we can pinpoint the wreck," the Coast Guard lieutenant was saying. "There have been only six on this bit of coast since 1885, and three of those, we know, were towed off for salvage purposes. Two others were steel freighters, sunk by submarines, and they lie rusting on the bottom a few miles offshore.

"That leaves us only one—the *Clara May*. She was a three-masted schooner out of Brunswick, Maine, carrying ice to the West Indies. She went down in the great blizzard of '88, a couple of miles south of the station. Only one man was saved—the cook. The old records of the Lifesaving Service don't show what happened to her afterward, but we presume she broke up somewhere out on the shoal. That would account for her keel being washed ashore in later storms and buried under the dune."

John Douglas looked puzzled. "All this happened long before we were born," he said. "And yet the timber and the figurehead seem to be sound and clean. Why haven't they been eaten by shipworms or covered with barnacles?"

"I think I have an answer for that," said Cameron with a nod. "A barnacle's a living salt-water animal—a shellfish, like an oyster. It has to be covered by the tide in order to feed. A teredo, or shipworm, is also a marine creature, and it only attacks wood that is under water. If the keel and stem of this schooner were washed ashore and buried under several feet of sand, above the normal tide line, they'd be well preserved for a long time.

"What I'm most interested in," he went on, "is getting more information about the *Clara May*—where she was built and when. Also, I'd like to know who carved our pretty lady here. I'll put in a call to a friend of mine at Bowdoin College. That's in Brunswick, the ship's home port. And now I'd better be moving if I want to get back to Princeton."

The discovery of the figurehead and all the work that followed it had put the Spanish dollar completely out of Don's mind. It wasn't until he put a hand in his pocket and felt it that he remembered. After the professor and the lieutenant had both left, he went into the little office where his father was busy on paper work.

"Dad," he said, "mind if I interrupt a minute? Here's something else I found on the beach today. Alec Cameron says it's a real Spanish piece of eight."

His father examined the heavy coin curiously. "So it is!" he exclaimed. "Did Cameron mention how old?"

"He said it was probably minted before 1700, and if I was lucky, I could get as much as twenty-five dollars for it."

John Douglas stroked his jaw. "You had quite a day of it, didn't you?" He chuckled. Then he became serious.

"I'd rather you didn't mention this coin to anybody else," he said. "One thing we don't need is a rush of treasure hunters digging up the island. So just put it away in a safe place. Later on I'll find out whether it's worth selling. Even if it isn't, you've got yourself a handsome keepsake."

Don found a spot at the back of his top bureau drawer, where he knew no one else was likely to look, and hid the coin there. Mrs. Douglas allowed the figurehead to remain in the living room overnight, but on Sunday after church, she insisted on having it removed. With the heavy timber it weighed well over a hundred pounds, and Don and his father had all they could do to carry it out to the tool house.

After that, all Don could do was wait for some word from Alec Cameron. Each day after school he went out and admired the sculptured head. He wondered whether the wood carver had modeled it after some real girl. If so, he thought, she must have been a beauty. Perhaps she was the actual Clara May for whom the ship had been named.

The Coast Guardsmen must have talked about finding part of the wreck, for most of the boys had heard the news at school. Miss Carter mentioned the matter in history class.

"I suppose there must have been many ships wrecked along the coast," she said. "Would you like to tell us about the one you found, Don?"

He recounted the details as Lieutenant Mason had given them. "I guess everybody's heard about the blizzard of '88," he said. "It must have been about the worst storm ever and terribly cold, too. It was a nor'easter with snow so thick no-body could see ten feet. This schooner was blown on the shoals and smashed up, and all hands lost but one. He told the lifesavers the ship's name and where she hailed from."

"What was her cargo?" Digger Jimson put in. "Was she carryin' gold?"

"No," Don replied. "It was ice."

A giggle ran through the class, but Miss Carter brought them to order. "Remember," she said, "that there was no electric refrigeration in those days. Down in the tropics ice was in great demand, and it made a profitable trade for New England vessels. Ice was cut in the Kennebec River during the winter and shipped south in the spring. That's how the *Clara May* happened to be off Topsail Island when she was caught by the blizzard."

Don waited till after class to speak to her. He was greatly impressed that Miss Carter knew so much about ships and their cargoes.

She laughed when he mentioned this. "I'm a Maine woman myself," she explained. "I grew up in Bath, where they built ships. Some day I'd like to come to Topsail and see that figurehead you found. It seems to me that's much more interesting than pirate treasure!"

EIGHT

Ocean Regional High continued to win its share of football games, and on Saturdays when they played at home, Don was there, rooting for the team. Bill Newton was one of the regular ends now and sure to win his letter.

It was well into November, but still no word had come from Alec Cameron about the schooner *Clara May*. Don wondered what would become of the beautiful figurehead. His father had warned him that some museum would probably want it, but in a way he still hoped he might be allowed to keep it.

From the marsh on the opposite side of the bay, the distant sound of guns came faintly each morning. The duck hunters were there in the blinds, firing into the flocks as they rose at dawn. John Douglas sent guards on patrol along the bay shore of the island, for the ducks and geese that sheltered there were a constant temptation to poachers.

On one Saturday, shortly before Thanksgiving, Don's mother was waiting for him at breakfast.

"No football game today, is there?" she said. "Well, that's good, because I want you to pick bayberries. If I'm going to make candles for Christmas presents, I'm going to need at least a bushel of nice berries."

"Aw, gee, Mom!" Don pleaded. "That's more'n a day's work!"

"Well, you can get me enough for a good start, anyway. I've been out for a look, and they're growing thick this year. If you stick to it, you shouldn't be more than four or five hours getting a bushel."

Don still grumbled a little, but within half an hour he was hiking down the road. He carried a big basket over his arm, and Bullet, the retriever, trotted along beside him. Actually Don didn't mind picking bayberries if they were plentiful and easy to find. He knew, too, how much his mother counted on his help in making her Christmas candles.

The thickest growth of bayberries on the island was about two miles south of the entrance gate. Visitors were forbidden to pick any flowers or other growing things, but John Douglas knew that no harm would come to the bushes if ripe bayberries were gathered in November. His only advice to Don was to keep out of sight of the road, in case any tourists were passing. Now that the season was over, even that possibility was remote.

Off to his right, the morning gunners were still to be heard on the other side of the bay. It would be a poor day for duckhunting, he thought, looking at the sky. The wind was too light and the weather too nice. It took cold, stormy mornings to stir up the flocks and bring the ducks in range of the blinds.

Don remembered from past years that a good patch of bayberry bushes lay just over the dune on the slope toward the bay. Calling the dog to follow, he scrambled across the crest of the ridge and saw nearly an acre of the waxy gray berries spread out before him. At the edge of the thicket, he started picking with both hands. Bayberries cling closer to the twigs than blueberries, and they were so much smaller that they filled the basket more slowly.

He stuck to it, working steadily for more than an hour.

Then his back ached from reaching into the bushes, and he decided it was time to take a break. Bullet had already left him. He could see the big brown dog nosing around out on the marsh.

Leaving his half-filled basket, Don went in the same direction. The tide was low enough to leave some of the flats exposed, and there were birds there, hunting food. Among them he picked out several gulls, a sanderling or two, and a longer-legged bird that he didn't recognize at first. Then he caught sight of the odd vertical striping of black and pale gray on its rear under parts and remembered seeing a picture of it in his book. It was, he was almost certain, a clapper rail —what the hunters called a "railbird."

Maybe, he thought, this was his reward for doing a good deed and picking bayberries. It had brought him another bird for his list. Though he hadn't brought his field glasses, he had a fairly good view of the large wader, and he stood there memorizing its shape, size, and coloring so that he could make a sure identification later.

"Don Douglas!" called a cheery voice behind him, and he turned quickly. At first he didn't think he knew the young woman coming down the slope. She wore green slacks, a sweater, and a leather jacket, and her blond hair was blowing in the light breeze. Then, as she came closer, she took off her sunglasses, and he recognized her.

"Hi, Miss Carter," he hailed her in return. "Why didn't you tell me you'd be coming today?"

"Just decided on the spur of the moment. Are you watching those gulls?"

"No, ma'am, not the gulls so much. There's another bird —a clapper rail—just this side of 'em. See the queer stripes on his underside? Looks as if he had on old-fashioned bathing trunks."

"Why, you're right." She laughed. "You seem to know quite a lot about birds."

He told her about the list he had made that autumn. "This one gives me forty-three," he said with pride.

"Look!" she cried, pointing out over the bay. "That big white bird is flying this way, and it seems to be in trouble!"

Don saw it then—a white goose, flapping awkwardly and losing altitude fast. One wing seemed to be damaged. It splashed into the water close to the shore.

"Hey, Bullet!" the boy yelled. "Go fetch!" And he pointed excitedly to the floundering goose.

The retriever didn't hesitate. He dashed across the flats and plunged into the water at full speed. Half a dozen vigorous strokes carried the dog within reach, and a moment later he was swimming back with the big bird's neck in his mouth.

"Oh!" cried Miss Carter. "He'll kill it!"

But when Bullet scrambled ashore and brought the goose to their feet, not a feather was disturbed.

"It's a snow goose!" Don exclaimed. "We don't see many around here. Some hunter on the mainland side shot at it. See? The wing's hurt—maybe broken."

He picked up the struggling creature and held it firmly in his arms, avoiding the frantic pecking of its beak.

"Have you got your car, Miss Carter?" he panted. "I've got to take this goose home and see if we can nurse her."

"Of course!" she replied. "I'm parked right up here on the road. Can you manage all right without getting eaten up?"

As they passed the bayberry patch, she picked up Don's basket, and they were soon in her little sedan on their way to the Douglas house.

"There's a big crate in the garage," Don said. "If I can get her into it, I guess she'll be safe until her wing heals up."

Miss Carter was helpful. She held onto the goose while Don hurried to bring out the crate and place it close to the back steps. Then, together, they put the huge squawking bird inside. The slats were two or three inches apart, and the goose immediately thrust her head through, hissing at her captors.

"What do you think she'll eat?" the history teacher asked.

"Corn, I guess. I'll ask my dad to get a big bag of it when he goes marketing this afternoon."

"Well," said Miss Carter, "the goose and I interrupted your bayberry picking. If I help, it won't take too long to fill the basket."

Mrs. Douglas had heard the commotion in the yard. Now she came out, and Don introduced her to Miss Carter. His mother was all hospitality at once and invited the teacher to have lunch with them. She wasn't quite as cordial to the goose.

"Where," she asked Don, "did you get this noisy thing?"

"It's a wild snow goose, Mom," he said. "Somebody shot at her and hurt her wing. She fell in the water, and Bullet brought her in. You don't mind if I take care of her, do you—please?"

It was hard for her to refuse anything in reason that her son asked. "All right," she agreed, "if your father doesn't mind. Now, if you're going back for more berries, don't forget we'll eat about twelve-thirty."

Miss Carter drove Don back to the bayberry patch, and they were soon picking side by side.

"What are you going to call your snow goose?" the teacher asked. "It seems as if she ought to have a name."

"Yes'm, I guess so. I sort o' thought I'd call her Amanda."

Miss Carter began to laugh while Don flushed with angry embarrassment.

76

"Forgive me," she said, "but it's really funny. Amanda's my own name. You wouldn't know because I always sign my papers just 'A. Carter.' "

"Gee!" Don stammered. "I wasn't trying to be funny. I—I just happened to think o' that name."

"It's all right." She chuckled. "I'm flattered, really. But let's not tell anyone else."

He went on picking for a while. "Don't you like to be called Amanda?" he asked. "I think it's a real pretty name."

"It sounds a little school-teacherish," she replied. "But tell me some more about your birds."

Don was glad to change the subject, and he gave her an enthusiastic account of the species he had seen. He also mentioned Alec Cameron, who had helped him so much with his list.

"Alec's going to find out more about the figurehead we dug up," he told her. "I'll show it to you when we get home."

"Good," said Miss Carter. "That's really why I came."

By noon they had filled the basket with bayberries and were back at the house. Don opened the tool-shed door, and there, in the shadows, stood the figurehead of the *Clara May*.

"Why," the teacher whispered, "she's lovely!"

She leaned forward and stroked the worn wood of the face. "That's Maine white pine," she told Don. "I can see the grain in the wood. It's wonderful stuff to carve."

"Lunchtime!" came Mrs. Douglas's call from the kitchen door. "Soup's on. Come and get it."

It was a pleasant meal, and when it was over, Miss Carter insisted on helping her hostess with the dishes. Don left them chatting there and went out to look at his patient in the crate. The goose appeared lively enough now. She flapped her good wing and stuck out her neck to hiss at him when he came too close. He found a tin pan, filled it with water, and set it outside the bars where she could reach it to drink. His father came by and grinned at the prisoner.

"Old lady," he said, "you don't look half as badly hurt as you pretend. Wait till I bring home a sack o' cracked corn, and we'll find out whether you've got any appetite."

When Amanda Carter came out, Don took her down to the dock to show her the boats. As they walked back, she asked him for more information about bayberry candles. "Aren't they very difficult to make?" she inquired. "I meant to ask your mother, but I forgot."

"Well, yes," he said. "I guess they're a lot o' work. But Mom doesn't mind, and they do make nice Christmas presents."

"I know the berries have a waxy feel," she said, "but how do you get the wax out?"

"We've got an old round-bottomed iron kettle," he explained. "We put the berries in it, a few handfuls at a time, and crush 'em with a wooden pestle. Then they're steamed with a little water in the kettle and a cover over it. It takes a while, but when they're done, the wax is pretty well out. Then we strain the whole mess to get the twigs an' dirt out of it and set it outside in the cold. The wax makes a layer on top, sort of a gray-green color. Mom skims it off and mixes it with regular paraffin for the candles, but the bayberry wax gives 'em some color and a nice smell."

"What about making the candles themselves?" she asked.

"First we dip wicks in the hot wax," said Don, "and hang 'em up to cool. Then the stiff, straight wicks are put in candle molds, and the wax is poured in around 'em. That's the part I can help with—that and picking the berries, o' course."

"Heavens!" The teacher laughed. "I was thinking of

making some myself, but I'm afraid I couldn't. No iron kettle, no candle molds."

"Oh, well," Don promised, "when the candles are made, I'll see that you get some for Christmas."

Just as Miss Carter was preparing to go home, a green Volkswagen drove in.

"Hey!" Don cried. "There's Alec Cameron now! Where've you been all this time, Alec?"

The professor looked brown and fit as he came toward them, smiling.

"Sorry, Don," he replied. "I'd have been here sooner, but I had to fly down to Caracas on a bird trip. Aren't you going to introduce me?"

Don made the introduction stumblingly. "Miss Carter's my history teacher," he explained. "She comes from Maine, and she's interested in our figurehead."

"I don't wonder," said Cameron. "I've heard from my Bowdoin College friend, by the way. There isn't much doubt that this is the figurehead of the schooner *Clara May*, and he says there was a famous wood carver in Brunswick by the name of Elijah Kittredge. Those initials you found are probably his—E. K."

"Of course!" Miss Carter exclaimed. "I didn't notice the initials, but I remember hearing of Mr. Kittredge when I was a little girl. He was supposed to make the prettiest figureheads on the whole coast of Maine."

The two knelt side by side to look more closely at the carving. Don hoped his two new friends would like each other.

From her crate, the goose Amanda made a plaintive honking gabble, and Don went over to comfort her. After a moment Cameron joined him there.

"What a beauty!" he said. "A snow goose! She's only

about the second one I've ever seen wild. There are a few in the larger zoos, but not many. Where'd you find her?"

"Miss Carter saw her trying to fly across the bay with a hurt wing. And it was Bullet that really saved her. You ought to have seen the way he brought her in!"

"Mind if I look at the wing?" asked the biologist.

With sure hands he explored the big bird's shoulder joint and the under part of the wing. "I don't think it's really broken," he said. "She caught some pellets of duck shot, though. Ought to be well in a week if you feed her and take care of her."

"You want to take a bird hike?" Don asked hopefully. "I saw a clapper rail today, and then Amanda, here—she makes forty-four on my list."

"I'd like to, Don," said Cameron with a grin. "But Miss Carter and I have just made a date for dinner over on the mainland. I'll come back and hike with you before too long, though."

Ten minutes later they were gone, and Don was left alone with the goose. It looked, he told himself, as if his wish about his friends had already begun to come true.

NINE

The mornings were frosty on the island those November days. Several times Don had to break a skim of ice on the water pan outside Amanda's crate. The snow goose didn't seem to mind her imprisonment. She ate every grain of the corn Don gave her twice a day, and from the way she flapped both her wings, he was sure the injured one was almost well. He hated to lose her, and yet his conscience told him she should be set free. The one question was whether she would be strong enough to overtake the rest of the flock, now far to the south.

John Douglas came out the back door two days before Thanksgiving and saw Don squatting in front of Amanda's cage.

"Hm," he said with a grin, "looks nice and fat, doesn't she? Maybe we won't need that turkey your mother's asked me to buy."

Don knew his father too well to rise to the bait. "That's right," he agreed mildly. "I might be willing to sell you the goose for a hundred dollars. Only don't expect me to eat any Thanksgiving dinner."

The superintendent chuckled. "Oh, well," he said, "it was just an idea that occurred to me. What do you intend to do with her? All that corn is costing me money."

"I haven't decided about her yet. She seems happy enough right here, but I know we can't keep her all winter."

The question was settled the next day when a letter came from Alec Cameron. "I have an offer for you from the Philadelphia Zoo," he wrote. "They need another snow goose and will pay $50 for the one you have. She'll be with other waterfowl in the big aviary, and I think she'll like it there. Anyhow, I'm driving over Saturday to see you, and you can decide then. If you're willing to sell, I can take her back with me."

"I think you'd better take the offer," said Don's mother. "Fifty dollars in your savings account will help with your college fund."

Don knew she was right. All that had worried him was the welfare of the goose, and having visited the Philadelphia Zoo, he remembered the spacious cage where the waterfowl lived. Amanda would have plenty of room to swim and to exercise her wings.

Thanksgiving brought a cold snap and a few flakes of snow. But inside the Douglas house all was snug, and the family made merry over a big dinner of turkey with all the appropriate side dishes. Later in the day when the sun came out, Don was pleased to see his friend Bill Newton coming up to the door.

"Haven't had much time for visiting this fall," Bill told him, "but now that football's over, I thought I'd hike down to Topsail. I wanted to see your white goose and that figurehead you found."

Don put on his winter jacket and took Bill out to the tool house. As they passed the crate, Amanda stuck her head out and squawked at the stranger.

"I don't know but what she's a better watchdog than old Bullet." Don laughed. "She won't be here long, though. Got a new home for her at the Philadelphia Zoo."

"Sure is pretty," said Bill. "I guess I never saw a snow

goose before. Those black tips on her wings sort o' dress her up, don't they?"

They went on to the shed where the figurehead was stored, and Don retold the story of the wreck of the *Clara May*.

"It's hard to believe the lady's eighty years old," he told his friend, "but there's the wood carver's date right on it. She's been buried under a lot o' sand, or she'd probably have rotted away by now."

"What do you plan to do with her?" Bill asked. "I bet a lot o' folks would like to see her."

"I know." Don nodded. "She ought to be on display somewhere. Maybe the County Historical Museum would take her. The way it is, if we stuck her outside for the tourists to see, she'd weather away in a few years."

"That storm must have really torn things up," Bill remarked. "Likely it uncovered a lot o' stuff that had been buried for years. Have you hunted for anything else—treasure, for instance?"

"Well, no," said Don, hesitating a little. "Not since we found the figurehead, that is."

"I bet young Digger Jimson has been out after buried pirate gold." Bill chuckled. "I saw him last Saturday night, when I went to the movies. I took Jane Williams. You know where she lives—down this side o' the Jimsons' place. After I'd brought her home and was heading up-island again about midnight, I saw Digger coming up from the dock with a lantern in one hand and a shovel in the other. Made me wonder where he'd been."

"That's right," Don replied. "Seems like a funny time o' night for him to be doing any digging. You reckon he'd been out in a boat?"

"No way to tell for sure, but it looked that way. It wasn't a clam rake he had. It was a regular garden spade."

Don was thoughtful. "You remember how sore Digger got in history class, that time we were talking about Captain Kidd?" he asked. "He was so sure there was treasure buried 'round here, you might think he'd seen it himself."

"Oh, well"—Bill laughed—"he could ha' been burying fishheads or garbage, I suppose. The way those folks live, they probably have a whole back yard full o' such stuff. Only thing was, I thought he was coming up from the dock."

After Bill had left, Don did some thinking. He remembered a number of odd happenings, such as the apparent landing of Fallon and Blake that evening when he had gone down the bay with his father.

"Hey!" he exclaimed to himself. "I never did ask if Dad found out about the registration on that Cadillac."

He brought the matter up that evening. "Dad," he asked, "did the State Police give you a run-down on the license o' that car Blake and Fallon were driving?"

"The Cadillac? Oh, sure, I thought I'd told you." John Douglas reached into a drawer of his desk and rummaged a moment.

"Here it is," he said, pulling out a slip of paper. "The car wasn't stolen, but it was registered in a different name. The owner is Stanislaus Balichek, Brooklyn, New York. Far as they could find, this Balichek doesn't have a police record, but I figure he's going under an assumed name—probably Blake. Who the little redhead really is, I don't know. What made you think of it?

"Nothing much," Don told him. "I just wondered, that's all."

*   *   *

The next day—Friday—was cold but clear. Don got up early and put on a sweater and windbreaker. He had no expectation of seeing any birds so late in the season, but he took his field glasses anyway and called Bullet to accompany him. The idea in his mind was to find out whether Digger Jimson had really been treasure hunting on Topsail Island.

His lack of exercise in the past month told on his bad leg, and at the end of the first two miles, he had to sit down on a driftwood log and rest. Energetically he rubbed the aching muscles and set out again. It was low tide, so he chose to hike along the hard sand rather than on the road. Bullet, however, roamed ahead, sometimes in the dunes, sometimes on the beach.

The only birds to be seen were herring gulls, congregated among the clamshells at the edge of the surf. Don's leg had loosened up a little with the steady exercise, and he kept on for more than an hour without stopping to rest. The Coast Guard station lay well behind him when he made his next halt. The sun was high in the southwest, and its warmth made him sweat. He opened his jacket and sat down, looking out to sea. Far off on the horizon, a big tanker was running up the coast, deep laden with oil for the Bayonne refineries. Otherwise, nothing moved except the restless waves.

Then somewhere a long way to the south, he heard Bullet barking. Sweeping the sky above the dune with his glasses, he looked for flying birds but could see none. The big dog, he thought, must have started a rabbit or some other land animal. He resumed his hike at a more leisurely pace, but Bullet kept on barking excitedly. Another sound reached him then—the sputter of an outboard motor being started.

Don went faster. He scrambled up the dune, pushing his way through trees and scrub. The retriever was down by the marsh now, his deep voice still rousing the echoes. And out in the bay a small outboard boat was rapidly heading northward. Don found it in his binoculars and was sure he recognized Digger Jimson alone at the tiller.

The dune he had just crossed was one of the highest on the island and covered with the thickest woods. There was one tree in particular that Don had noticed before—a huge old cedar, its gnarled trunk close to three feet in diameter. The gales of many winters had twisted its limbs and kept it from growing very tall, but there was no question about its great age.

Don whistled for the dog to rejoin him, then returned to the big tree. Bullet came panting up and immediately started sniffing around the cedar's roots. Then he whined and pointed his nose at a chip of wood in the sand. Don stooped and picked it up. A shred of cedar bark clung to the back, and it appeared to have been sliced from the tree with a knife.

Moving slowly around the trunk, Don looked for some sign of a cut. Perhaps he was wrong, and the chip had come from a different tree. Then, about four feet above the ground, he found a grayish spot, lighter than the brown of the bark. It glistened as if it were wet, and when he touched a finger to it, a gray stain came off on his skin. He took his knife and scraped at the spot. Sure enough, under the stain there was the white wood of a fresh cut.

Don stood there puzzled. He wouldn't have been surprised to catch young Jimson digging in the sand for treasure or even doing a bit of poaching for ducks if any had been around. But there seemed to be no explanation for what he had found. Except for the gray paint, he would have said the cut on the tree was an ordinary blaze, such as a Boy Scout might make to mark a trail. But why this particular big cedar, and why a blaze at all, when the woods were confined to a strip a hundred feet wide along the top of the dune?

After a lot of thinking that brought him to no logical answer, Don looked at his watch. It was well after eleven o'clock, and he was a long way from home. He called Bullet and started hiking up the road.

His bad leg was giving him trouble before he was halfway to the head of the island. That was understandable, for he knew he had tramped at least eight miles southward and another three or four on the return trip. It was a longer walk than he had attempted since the early autumn.

Resting beside the road, he was relieved to hear the sound of an approaching car. It was his father, driving the pick-up truck, and when Don waved to him, he pulled to a stop.

"Your mother was a bit worried when you didn't get home at noon," the superintendent said. "Hop in and I'll give you a lift. How far down did you go, anyhow?"

"A couple o' miles south o' the Coast Guard station," Don replied. "Dad, you know that big cedar tree in the woods on top o' the dune?"

"I reckon so. Real big old tree?"

"That's the one. How long do you think that cedar's been there?"

"Shucks—how does anybody know? I'd guess three hundred years. It's certainly the oldest tree on Topsail. Why? What made you ask?"

Don didn't answer for a second. He needed to think about it a little more. "Nothing much," he mumbled. "I just noticed how big it was and wondered if it wasn't pretty old."

"Well, it's been around a long time—back to early colonial days and maybe longer. I wouldn't want anything to happen to that tree. After a big storm I usually go down there to make sure it's still standing. It's a landmark I'd hate to lose."

Don ate the lunch that had been kept for him, then retreated to his room. He knew his leg needed rest and lay down on his bed for a while. There he got to thinking once more about buried treasure. In every story that dealt with pirate gold, he remembered there had to be a map. It might be a crudely drawn map, made with a charred stick or even a finger dipped in blood. But it indicated the position of the treasure by telling how many paces to go from some given point and in what direction.

That was it—you had to have some kind of landmark from which to start! In most tales it was a peculiarly shaped rock or a boulder with a secret mark on it. But here on the Jersey coast there were no rocks—only sand, constantly shifting with wind and tide.

It was his father's description of the old cedar as a "landmark" that had started Don thinking. If it was actually as much as three hundred years old, it would have been a good-sized tree when Captain Kidd sailed the seas!

Don felt a glow of excitement, as if he were getting close to something. Then it died as he realized that Digger Jimson probably knew the island as well as he did and would have no need to put a blaze on the big cedar to identify it. Most baffling of all was the gray stain covering the fresh-cut wood. He was as much in the dark as ever.

About four o'clock that afternoon Don got up, stretched his stiff muscles, and went to the table where he did his homework. There were still a few pages of the history assignment to be read, and he settled down with his book. Before he had sat there five minutes, a faint sound came to him through the closed window. It was disturbing only because he didn't know exactly what it was.

He went to the window and pushed up the sash. Then as he listened, it came once more—a sweet, soft honking high in the sky. Not Canada geese, he thought, for their voices were hoarser and deeper. These notes sounded high-pitched, almost like elfin music. Don seized the field glasses and hurried out to the dooryard.

It took only a moment for him to pick out a V-formation of flying birds, miles away in the western sky above the bay. He worked on the focus of the binoculars until he was able to see individual birds in the group. They were white, with long necks stretched straight out before them, and though they were far away, he was certain of their great size. Then he knew! He had sighted a late flight of whistling swans, winging south to their winter home in the Carolina sounds!

Adding another bird to his list was a pleasure he hadn't foreseen. Now, counting carefully once more, he found he had a total of forty-five. And later on, when the spring migration got under way, he was sure he could pick up still more.

That night he wrote a note to Alec Cameron describing the swan flight he had heard and seen. At the end he said: "If you have time some weekend soon, I hope you can come down to the island. There's a mystery here that I can't make head or tail of, and I'd like to talk to you about it."

Once the letter was deposited in the R.F.D. box, he was able to shake off his worries. There was nothing to do but wait now and discuss the puzzle with the professor. Somehow he was confident that his friend would be able to figure out an answer.

On Saturday Don did no more hiking, for the weather was cold and blowy with a threat of snow. Instead, he helped his mother with the candlemaking. All day the kitchen was fragrant with pungent steam as they tried out the bayberry wax, and by nightfall there was a row of sixty candles, fresh from the molds, cooling on a long shelf.

"Smells good and Christmasy 'round here," said John Douglas when he came in at suppertime. "By the way, Don, those two fellows in the Cadillac are back at Jimsons'. I saw their car there as I drove by."

TEN

"Don," said Miss Carter as he was leaving her history class one day the following week, "could you stop in a minute after school?"

"Why, sure, Miss Carter. Just so I don't miss the bus."

She laughed. "If it leaves without you, I'll have an excuse to drive you down to Topsail. Don't forget, now."

After his last class, he reported to her room and found her looking at an old leather-bound book.

"I thought you'd be interested in this, Don," she said with a smile. "I wanted to know more about the Indians along the coast, and at the County Library I found this book. It's a history of the Lenni Lenape tribe, who used to hunt and fish in New Jersey a few hundred years ago. Have you ever found any Indian relics on the island?"

"You mean like arrowheads and stuff? No, ma'am, I haven't."

"Well," she replied, "I doubt if they did any hunting except on the mainland, so there wouldn't be any arrowheads along the beach. But this book says Topsail Island was a favorite place for getting clams and oysters, especially down near the inlet at the lower end. How would you like to do some exploring with me down there? I could make it this Saturday if you're not busy."

"Sure—I'd like that," he told her with a grin. "Come in the morning, and I'll tell Mom you'll be there for lunch."

The history teacher came as promised. At nine o'clock on Saturday, her Falcon car stopped in front of the house, and Don hurried out to join her.

"Aren't we lucky?" she asked gaily. "The day's so warm and sunny, I'd almost like to go for a swim!"

Don chuckled. "Know what the water temperature was last night?" he asked. "Thirty-nine! I heard it on the radio."

"Well," she replied ruefully, "I guess that *is* a little too cold. But anyway, it's a fine day for exploring."

They reached the inlet half an hour later, after stopping for a moment near the big cedar.

"Dad says he reckons that tree was here more than three hundred years ago," Don explained. "If he's right, then the Indians must have seen it on their way up and down the island. Or do you figure they used to come over here by canoe?"

"Oh"—she laughed—"let's say they did see the tree. I expect, though, that back in those days there were bigger trees all around it. They had to cross the bay in canoes. There wasn't any other way to get here."

They parked the car near the surf-casting area, now deserted, and walked westward along the shore of the inlet. The incoming tide was meeting a sharp west wind and kicking up a heavy chop. A few herring gulls wheeled and screamed above the waves, looking for fish, but not a human being was to be seen.

"Don," said Miss Carter, "it must have looked exactly like this when the Lenni Lenape were here!"

"Maybe not," Don told her practically. "The shore keeps changing every year, and the inlet might have been a mile further south in those days."

"What I meant," she explained, "was that all they saw was sand and sea and fishing gulls. What do you suppose that little white hill is over toward the bay side?"

"I never looked close. Just a pile o' white sand, I guess."

"Let's find out," she answered, and together they went toward the white knoll. As they came nearer, Don was surprised to see it was made of shells—broken clam and oyster shells, bleached by sun. There must have been tons of them in the pile.

"Gosh!" Don exclaimed. "Where'd they all come from? Looks like there are millions of 'em!"

"I think," said Miss Carter, "there's only one way they could have come here. The book I showed you says that for many years one of the smaller tribes of the Lenni Lenape came here to dry clams and oysters for winter food. Two or three hundred of them—braves, squaws, and papooses— would paddle over from the mainland and camp in the dunes. It usually happened in the hot months when it was cool and pleasant by the sea. The men spent their time gathering shellfish, while the women opened them and dried the meat in the sun, then smoked it over slow fires."

"Hm," said Don. "I can see how they could dig clams with a stick, but what about the oysters? They didn't have oyster tongs, did they?"

"I doubt if they did. But the Indian boys were good swimmers, and they used to dive to the oyster beds and pick up the oysters in their hands. You can see how the empty shells must have piled up over the years."

Don climbed to the top of the shell heap. From that vantage point, he could see the broad tide flats on the western shore of the island, which would probably provide good clamming. Then he looked north, along the brush-covered ridge of the dunes. It wasn't hard to imagine large trees growing there and the skin tents of the Indians set up among them.

Coming down, he found a driftwood stick and used it to start digging at the base of the shell pile. The fragments had been welded together by centuries of water, wind, and sun till they formed a mass almost as hard as rock. If any Indian relics were buried there, they weren't likely to be found.

For a moment the thought crossed his mind that there might be some connection here with Digger Jimson's activities. But no—all Digger wanted was pirate gold. Blake, or Balichek, and his red-haired companion had been down at this end of the island, but again he doubted if they knew or cared anything about Indians.

With Miss Carter, he did a little more exploring in the dunes and down along the inlet shore, but no more discoveries turned up.

"Well," the teacher said with a laugh, "we'll have something to tell the history class, at least. Or you could write a theme for English—about the first summer visitors to Topsail Island!"

Don's father was at home when they arrived for lunch, and he was interested in their account of the morning's activities.

"The old shell mound's still there, is it?" he asked. "I explored the place years ago, but I guess I never showed you the Indian things I found."

When he rose from the table, he went up to the attic and brought down several stone implements. The smallest one Don recognized at once as a broken arrowhead. But there were also a long tapered piece of flint, which his father called the point of a fish spear, and a heavy, blunt stone axhead.

"That's not a tomahawk," Don's father explained. "Too heavy and not sharp enough. But you can see where a ring has been chipped away here, so it could be tied to the handle with a thong. One man who saw it said it was a 'warhawk'—a heavy club they used in battle."

"Gee, Dad," said Don, "I didn't know you had these things. Maybe we ought to start a little Indian museum to show the tourists. Anyhow, please don't put 'em away in the attic. I'd like to take 'em to school if you don't mind. Lots of kids have arrowheads, but I bet there aren't many who ever saw a real warhawk!"

* * *

No letter came from Alec Cameron until the second week in December. When he wrote at last, it was to say he had been very busy classifying specimens from South America but would try to drive down to Topsail the following weekend.

Meanwhile, with his father's approval, Don put the Indian relics in a stout box and carried them to school. Miss Carter was delighted. In history class that afternoon, she showed the articles one by one and described their use.

Digger Jimson was scornful of the little collection. "Heck!" he said. "I've got a dozen arrowheads better'n that one!"

"Fine," Miss Carter told him with a smile. "Why don't you bring them in, so we can put them on display? And you other boys—don't you have some Indian things to contribute? We could put a card with each one, telling the name of the owner."

Several answered eagerly that they would bring what they had.

"I never found any," Bill Newton put in, "but I've got a good idea. Last fall my dad was remodeling McCord's candy store, and there were a couple of old glass cases nobody wanted. They're in our carpenter shop now, just gathering dust. S'pose I borrow the truck an' bring one in. It'd make a good display case to show off our collection."

By Friday of that week the case had been cleaned and polished and set up at one side of the room. In it were more than fifty different pieces, mostly in the form of arrowheads and small ax blades. But there were also two stone bowls, Don's warhawk, and a curious Indian fishhook made from the bone of a large bird. What made the class proudest, however, were the neatly lettered cards, giving credit to those who had loaned their relics.

The display stayed there for more than a month and was visited by nearly every student in the school.

On Saturday, as he had promised, Alec Cameron arrived shortly after noon. "I'll have to be back at college this evening," he told Don, "but I want to help you if I can. What's bothering you, son?"

"Well," Don replied, "it'll be easier to explain if I show you something. Let's drive down the island a way."

When they reached the big cedar on the dune, he asked Alec to park the car. As they climbed through the sand and brush, he started to tell his story.

"First of all," he said, "how old do you think that tree is?"

"Hard to tell," the professor answered, "unless we could drill out a core and count the rings. But it's certainly a big tree, considering all the storms it's had to endure. At a guess, I'd say over two hundred years."

Don nodded. "Dad says three hundred, but it doesn't matter much. Now come up close and see if you notice anything odd about it."

Cameron moved slowly around the trunk till he came to the gray-stained blaze. "What happened here?" he asked.

"Looks as if it had been cut with a knife, but it seems to be weathered."

"No," Don told him, "just stained. I found it when the gray was still wet."

"I see now," said the biologist. "A really old scar would have a ridge of bark on all sides where the tree had grown out around it. This seems to be a clumsy attempt to make it *look* old, though I guess it would fool nine people out of ten."

"I'm pretty sure I know who did it," Don went on. "There's a boy my age named Digger Jimson. He lives on the upper island, and his dad rents boats for bay fishing and sells bait. I just caught a glimpse of him leaving when I noticed the cut. He may have been put up to it by a couple o' strangers who have been hanging around. One is a big, heavy-set, black-haired guy, who calls himself Blake. The other one's smaller and red-headed, and he gave his name as Fallon. But when Dad had the State Police check on the license of the Cadillac they drive, they found it's registered to a Mr. Balichek, of Brooklyn. We're pretty sure the name Blake is an alias."

"You say they've been on the island? What were they doing?"

Don told about their disappearance from the beach, then described seeing them come up the bay in one of Jimson's boats. "Their car's been parked at Jimson's other times, too," he added. "Another queer thing is what makes young Digger so sure there's pirate treasure buried down here. At school he claimed his family had rented boats to someone who knew just where the gold was."

Cameron stroked his jaw thoughtfully. "I don't wonder you feel puzzled," he said with a grin. "The evidence certainly seems to point to mischief of some kind. But if it was merely a matter of young Jimson and his two dubious friends hunting for treasure on the island, why on earth should the boy blaze a tree? More than that, why should he try to conceal the blaze with gray paint? It's really quite a mystery you've got here, my boy!"

Together they searched the strip of woods and the west side of the sandy dune, down as far as the marsh. There were no more clues to be found, and of course no footprints were left in the loose sand. Don did discover a stake driven into the mud at the edge of a little tidal creek, and they both agreed that must have been where Digger had tied his boat. Don looked especially for any sign that a shovel had been used, but the dune and the flats were just as they had been for years.

"Well," said Alec Cameron, "I'm afraid I'll have to go back now. But let me mull over it a bit. I'll let you know if I get any good ideas. It's this pair, Blake and Fallon, that interest me most. Your young friend Digger is probably just carrying out their orders. Remember to keep me posted if there are any new developments."

After the Volkswagen had departed across the bridge, Don went up to his room and carefully put down on paper all he knew or suspected about the mystery. That, he had read, was the way famous detectives worked. But it didn't seem to do any good, no matter how hard he studied the list.

Perhaps there was something he had left out—some insignificant fact that would be the key to all the rest. He racked his brains without discovering anything more. At last, he stuck the paper in a drawer and decided to forget the whole business unless some new incident occurred.

The Sunday paper was delivered the next morning, but it was after dinner that afternoon before the family had a chance to read it. Don was on the floor with the color comics when he heard his father chuckle.

"Here's an item that ought to interest you, Don," the superintendent remarked. "It's headed: 'EXPERTS DIVIDED OVER CAPT. KIDD'S LOG.' It says an old manuscript has turned up with the pirate's own private account of what he did with his treasure. But the scholars can't agree whether the thing is real or a fake."

"May I read it when you're done?" asked Don eagerly.

"Sure—go ahead," his father told him, and tossed the paper in his direction.

It was a fairly long article, Don found. Under the headline, the story read as follows:

Is the ancient yellowed parchment that Mr. Kurt Falkenhein claims he found in the attic of a very old Long Island farmhouse genuine or a remarkable forgery?

That is the question being hotly argued by savants in a number of New York museums and universities. Tests of the paper and ink have been made by at least two analytical chemists, and they, too, hold different views. One says it's a fraud. The other is equally certain that the manuscript dates back to the late seventeenth century.

In any case, the discovery raises interesting questions regarding the loot collected by the notorious Captain William Kidd in his years of buccaneering. Most historians have believed his only treasure was recovered on Gardiner's Island, near the eastern tip of Long Island, soon after Kidd was hanged in 1701. It amounted to 14,000 pounds sterling—nearly $60,000 in present-day

American money. However, there have always been those who scoffed at the idea, claiming that Kidd was known to have robbed ships of many times that sum. And this log of his activities appears to suggest what he actually did with the gold and jewels. Allowing for the odd spelling of words and the strange punctuation, the gist of the manuscript follows.

ELEVEN

Don's eyes were fairly popping as he curled up on the rug and devoured every word of the message from long ago. He read:

Ye Pryvate Log of Wm. Kidd, Captayn

Not knowing where or when I may be taken in Custody, I wish to sett downe ye Factes conserning my Activityes in ye past three Yeres. Bearing ye King's Commission I sett sayle in ye Galley *Adventure* from Plymouth England in 1696. My purpose was to Capture Pyrate vessels in ye Indian Ocean off Madagascar. Many fell under ye Attackes of my Crew and great store of Treasure was taken.

In 1698 ye Men mutinyed and sayled off a-pyrating in ye *Adventure* leaving me Ashore. But I hidd and kept by me ye Chest with most of ye Gold and Precious Stones. After two Monthes I was able to secure a small Sloop and three men to sayle her. We had a long and stormey Voyage around ye Cape of Goode Hope and Northerly to New Yorke. Arryving near ye Harbour, ye news came to me that I was to be Hunted as a Pyrate.

Making all Speed we set Sayle again and cruised about one hundred mile till we found a desert Island where no men dwelt. There I carryed ye Chest ashore with one man to dig ye Sand. When ye Hole was a fathom deepe we lowered ye Treasure in and I buryed ye seaman upon ye Chest with a Pistol bullet in his Head. Ye otheres heard ye Shot and mayde off with ye Sloop. I was Forced to Swim to ye Mayne Land and walk all ye way hither.

Synce I am Lyke to come soon to Tryal I have drawn a Mappe to Show ye Spotte where ye Chest is hid, and this I will give to ye Only Person I can Surely Trust.

I call Heaven to my Witnesse I am Innocent of ye Charges brought against me. Signed this 20th day of Maye, 1699,   Wm. Kidd, Capt.

Don drew a deep breath. "Dad," he said, "did you read it all?"

"Why, sure. It sounds like a pretty wild idea, doesn't it?"

"The island!" Don choked. "It was about a hundred miles by sea from somewhere around New York. An uninhabited island, too! Could be Topsail, couldn't it?"

His father grinned, then grew serious. "Maybe," he said, "or Barnegat, or somewhere in the other direction, up the New England coast. Anyhow, don't get any wild ideas, son. Sooner or later they'll prove it's a fake, like a lot of other such manuscripts. I suppose we've got to watch out for people who figure it the same way you did, though. I'd better tip off the gate guards."

Don felt a bit let down, but he was still excited by what he had read. He cut the article out of the paper and took it upstairs to place with his notes. In some way he was sure it fitted in with what he already knew. One thing especially intrigued him. Who was this man called Kurt Falkenhein? It sounded like a foreign name, German, perhaps. He wished the Sunday paper had carried a picture of him, for he couldn't help feeling he might recognize the man if he saw him.

Christmas was coming soon, and that last week of school before vacation the students did more skylarking than work. Don noticed that Digger Jimson was even cockier than usual. In history class Miss Carter had to reprimand him for talking and laughing while she was giving out assignments.

"That's all right, ma'am," he replied with a snicker. "I was just tellin' my friends how wrong you was about Cap'n Kidd's treasure. Or don't you read the papers?"

She flushed but kept her temper. "Richard," she said, "I'm sure you'd like to apologize for that remark. I'd be sorry to have to send you to the principal's office."

He mumbled an apology, and the incident was over for the moment, at least. But in the bus on the way home, he had plenty to say.

"Guess I told old Carter off!" he crowed. "Maybe she don't read the Sunday papers. If she did, she'd know Cap'n Kidd *did* bury his gold—right down here on Topsail Island, too!"

Don, who should have known enough to keep his mouth shut, rose to Miss Carter's defense. "That story in the paper didn't prove a thing," he answered hotly. "It's likely a fake anyhow, but if it's true, the treasure could be any place from Nantucket to Cape May."

"Why, you one-legged squirt!" Jimson snarled. "You're nothin' but a teacher's pet—an' chicken, too!"

He reached over and gave Don a shove that knocked him against the girl in the seat beside him. Don's temper flared at that. He sprang up and seized Digger by the collar, jerking him into the aisle. In another second, he had him in a head-lock and wrestled him to the floor of the swaying bus.

For all his lameness, Don had strong arms, and for a moment he was able to hold his wiry opponent down. Then Digger twisted loose and jumped away, brandishing his fists.

"I oughta kill you, you lousy runt!" he raged.

Don tried to get up, but a jolt of the bus made his leg collapse under him. As Jimson danced toward him, he sat there with tears of anger and frustration running down his cheeks. Then Bill Newton grabbed Digger and slammed him back into the nearest seat.

The driver put on his brakes, bringing the bus to a lurching stop. "You kids cool it back there," he shouted, "or I'll signal the next police car to run you in!"

Bill helped Don get back on his feet and into his seat.

"Go ahead, skipper," he told the driver cheerfully. "The ruckus is all over, and I'll see it stays that way."

There were no more incidents on the trip. As they approached Jimson's stop, he swaggered down the aisle with a scornful look at his late adversary. Don had calmed down by that time. He was the last to get off, and the driver gave him a grin as he passed.

"Don't blame you for gettin' sore," he remarked. "That kid had it comin' to him after some o' the things he said. You all right now? Didn't get hurt, did you?"

"Naw," said Don. "I'm O.K., thanks. See you tomorrow."

As he hiked homeward across the bridge, his anger returned, but this time it was directed against himself. If he hadn't flared up when Digger started ridiculing Miss Carter, the other boy might have said more—let drop some information that would help solve the puzzle of the blazed tree. As it was, Don had learned nothing more than he knew before. There was no excuse, he thought bitterly, for being so stupid.

*   *   *

Almost before Don realized it, Christmas was just around the corner. He had helped his mother pack the gift candles and wrap them in bright-colored paper, making sure one package was for Miss Carter. Then he set about buying presents for his family. The first day of the Christmas vacation, he rode with his father to the upper island and made a round of the stores in the shopping center. He knew his father needed a new sweater, and in a good men's store he found a handsome cardigan in John Douglas's size. Finding a gift for his mother was a lot harder. At last he chose a little brass kettle with some bright artificial flowers in it. By the time he got back to the car, he had spent all the allowance he had been saving for three months. But he was proud of the nicely wrapped packages that he carried.

The day before Christmas was calm and clear, with the thermometer up to fifty degrees. In the afternoon Don took his field glasses and went down to the beach to watch the herring gulls. A light breeze blew off the land, and the sea was so calm that many of the gulls were floating on the waves.

He found an old timber where he could sit and watch the big gray and white birds. They were awkward enough on land but graceful in the air or on the water. After half an hour, he was about to move on when he happened to notice a smaller swimmer, black on the head and back and with a white breast. Its black tail was cocked upward jauntily. He trained the binoculars on it and was startled to see a huge thick bill, all black except for a vertical white stripe. Don was excited. This was certainly a new bird for his list, but what was it? He had no notebook with him today. All he could do was try to remember each detail and hurry home to find the stranger in his bird book.

Once he came to the picture, there was no doubt about the

identification. What he had seen was a razor-billed auk. Carefully he added the name to his census—his forty-sixth bird! He was tempted to rush off a post card to Alec Cameron with the news, but there was no telling where the biologist might be spending his holidays.

That evening he went to sing carols with the young people of the church and didn't get to bed till an hour after midnight. When he woke the next morning, he rolled over and tried to go back to sleep. Then, realizing it was Christmas Day, he hurried into his clothes and went down to breakfast.

The gaily wrapped gifts were ready to be opened. Both his parents were very appreciative of his presents. And when he opened his own main gift and found a fine microscope, his joy knew no bounds. It was a real precision instrument, even more powerful than the ones in the high-school laboratory.

There were a hundred things he wanted to examine under the lens. One of his first actions was to dash down to the beach and pick up a stray feather from a gull's wing and a handful of sand. These kept him happily occupied most of the morning.

Each grain of sand, he found, was completely different from the others—as individual as the features of a human being. Some were minute bits of stone, ground and polished to round or oval shapes, hardly bigger than the point of a pin. Others had evidently been broken off more recently and still had rough edges and corners. But what surprised him most was that well over half the grains were bits of shell rather than of rock. He almost fancied he could tell whether they came from clams or oysters or the thinner shells of crabs.

Still more fascinating was the gull feather. First he cut a small section of the hollow quill and marveled at its strength in proportion to its light weight. No human engineer had ever conceived a more perfect material for an air-borne structure.

Next, with a pair of his mother's tweezers, he began separating the barbs that grew out of the shaft. When he placed a tiny segment of one under the microscope, he discovered other still smaller "barbules" spreading from it in an intricate network that made the surface of the feather appear unbroken. Each of these hairlike barbules looked as fragile as a snow crystal. Yet they formed a fabric strong enough to lift a bird's body!

Don was so absorbed that he had to be called twice for dinner, and even then he left the instrument with regret. No Christmas gift he had ever received had given him such enjoyment. He told his family about his discoveries enthusiastically, and finally he tried to call his science teacher, Garry Reynolds, on the telephone. As he feared, Reynolds had gone home to Pennsylvania for the holidays, and he had to content himself with drawing the wing structure as it appeared under the lens. In the evening he showed the picture to his father and asked him to guess what it was. John Douglas studied it for a while.

"Looks like a fern," he said, "or a piece of very fine lace."

When Don told him, he was considerably impressed. "You know," he exclaimed, "that was the right present for you! I wouldn't be a bit surprised if you do turn out to be a scientist!"

For the next few days, Don stayed glued to the microscope, except when he was out gathering fresh specimens to examine. He studied the layers of a broken clamshell, a hair from his own head and one from Bullet's rough coat, the wing of a dead wasp he found in the attic, and a tiny wisp of wool from the living-room rug.

At last he realized that he needed exercise. The final

day of December was cloudy and raw but not too cold for hiking, and he took his binoculars and started down the road. He had whistled for Bullet, but the retriever was off somewhere exploring on his own.

This time Don saw no strange birds along the beach. The gulls, for the most part, sat huddled on the sand, facing the chill wind.

When he reached the Coast Guard station, he stopped to get warm and pass the time of day with his friend Tom Coleman. The young seaman gave him a cup of steaming coffee and asked about the figurehead he had helped salvage from the dune.

"She's still sitting in our tool shed," Don told him. "I know that's no place for her, but so far no museum has asked for her."

Coleman nodded. "Too bad," he said. "Sure is a handsome piece o' carvin'. By the way, have you or your father been down the island at night lately?"

"Not that I know of. Why?"

"I was on patrol in the jeep the other night, an' about two miles below here, I thought I saw a light movin' back o' those thick woods. I stopped an' watched the place, but it was all dark after that, so I figured I'd been mistaken."

"Gee," said Don, "I wish you'd called Dad up. I bet there *was* somebody down there. We've sort of expected there'd be some treasure hunters fooling around on the island. Did you see that story in the Sunday paper about Captain Kidd?"

"I didn't read it, but I heard some o' the fellers mention it—just kiddin' o' course. Said they planned to find all that gold an' retire rich."

Don nodded. "I don't know why everybody thinks it's here," he replied. "All Kidd said in that paper he's supposed to have left was that it was buried on a deserted island about a hundred miles from New York. I reckon the folks at Beach Haven an' Montauk are just as stirred up as they are 'round here. Anyhow, my father figures the whole thing is a hoax."

"Well," said Coleman, "we'll keep our eyes peeled. O' course, keepin' folks off the island is your dad's job, not ours. But we'll let him know if anything happens."

TWELVE

Don kept on walking down the road till he came to the wooded dune and the big cedar tree. All was quiet there now except for the moaning of the winter wind in the branches. He went carefully around the tree, looking for any sign of further trespassing, but found nothing at all. Suddenly, the stillness was broken by the harsh cawing of a crow. It must have been watching him from a treetop and now decided to warn the neighborhood that an enemy was present.

As the big black bird flapped away over the marsh, Don wondered whether it would be fair to include it in his list. Why not? It was as much an inhabitant of the island as a redwing blackbird, and he had often seen crows on the beach, picking over crabshells for bits of food. Besides, he knew there was a species known as the fish crow, and for all he could tell, this might be one. Number forty-seven!

He went on through the brush and down the western slope of the dune. There, a few yards from the edge of the marsh, the sand seemed to have been disturbed. It was hard to tell what had happened there, but it looked suspiciously as if a small area of sand had been dug up and then replaced. Don didn't know just why he thought so, but somehow the surface didn't look quite natural.

Turning northward, he followed the contour of the dune

and came to another spot that looked slightly wrong to him. In all, during the next half hour, he found five places where he believed some digging had been done.

When Don started home, he began to realize that after a week of inactivity, he was out of condition. His leg had stiffened and the muscles felt tired. By the time he hobbled up to the Coast Guard station, he knew he would have to get a ride somehow.

The yeoman on duty in the front office was a stranger, but when he asked to use the phone, the man was cordial enough about it. Don dialed his home and found his father was away. At that point the yeoman interrupted.

"Are you the superintendent's son?" he asked. "I reckon you want a lift up the island, and the patrol car's due by here right now. They'll be glad to take you home."

When the jeep arrived, the man at the wheel turned out to be Tom Coleman. As they rode, Don told him about the places he had found where digging seemed to have been done.

"You know," said the young seaman, "that must ha' been what was goin' on when I saw the light that night. They must ha' heard me stop or spotted my headlights. So they beat it out o' there. But like I told you, we'll keep a close watch on the place."

That evening Don talked to his father. "Somebody's been digging in the dunes down there back o' the big cedar," he said. "And Tom Coleman says he saw a light there late one night. Don't you think we ought to set a guard over the place?"

John Douglas laughed. "I guess if anyone's been there, it was just kids," he said. "Maybe your young friend Jimson. But keeping a guard would be mighty expensive. These men who work for the State Park Service aren't soldiers.

They'd want double pay for overtime if they were willing to do it at all. Anyhow, I doubt if that kind of trespassing is likely to turn into an epidemic. It might be years before they come back."

Don knew his father made sense. In a way he was disappointed, but he was more determined than ever to get to the bottom of the mystery.

New Year's passed, and all too soon Don was back in school again. He had hoped to talk to Bill Newton about what he had found, but Bill was out to make the basketball team and took a later bus home.

The mail was on the table when Don entered the house that afternoon. He needed only a glance to spot the familiar handwriting of Alec Cameron on an envelope addressed to him.

There was a clipping enclosed with the letter. Cameron wrote that he had seen the story in a New York tabloid and was sending it on for Don to read. He also promised to come to the island the next weekend if he could get away. Don opened the clipping and read:

NEW EVIDENCE POINTS
TO CAPT. KIDD'S TREASURE
Was Hester Winters the "One Person"
the Pirate Could Trust?

New York, Dec. 28. A reporter for this newspaper has located the house where Captain William Kidd's famous "Private Log" was discovered. It is a very old house, not presently occupied, said to have been built in 1690, on the south shore of Long Island not far from Sayville. Here, according to legend, lived a mysterious woman named Hester Winters. Little is known of her, except that rumor tells of frequent visitors from the sea, usually coming by night.

Our reporter obtained access to the house and explored it thoroughly. There were evidences that it had recently been ransacked from attic to cellar, but he found one interesting clue that the earlier searchers seemed to have missed. In a dark corner of the attic, under a pile of rags, was a letter, dusty and yellowed with age. It was addressed in a bold hand to "Mistress H. Wynters," and the seal had been broken. On the inner surface, in faded ink, was written: "Will be Comyng Before ye Weake is Out. W. K."

Careful examination by antiquarians proves this note to be at least 200 years old and probably older. There can be little doubt that it was written by the notorious Captain Kidd.

The discovery of the note gives added weight to the authenticity of the "Log" which Mr. Kurt Falkenhein says he found in the same house—the house of Captain Kidd's friend, Hester Winters! But what became of the "Mappe" Kidd mentions in his Log? Unless those who searched the house before Mr. Falkenhein located the priceless chart, Kidd's treasure must still remain a mystery.

*　　*　　*

Don's forehead was wrinkled with thought as he read the item over again and studied the fuzzy picture of the note. It seemed to him almost too much of a coincidence that a second document should suddenly turn up, "proving" what was in the first. But the map itself was still missing. How long would it be before someone found it, he wondered?

And what about the mysterious Mr. Falkenhein? If he had the map, would he tell the world where the treasure was buried? Not much of a chance of that, Don thought. He was probably keeping his secret and preparing to dig up the gold himself.

On Friday came a fairly heavy rain mixed with sleet—as miserable a day as they had had all winter. Don came home from school dripping water off his slicker and sou'wester. If the storm kept on, he doubted whether Alec Cameron would be coming the next day.

But the weather changed abruptly about six that night. John Douglas came in stamping his feet and rubbing his hands.

"Brrr, it's cold!" he exclaimed. "Cold front's come through, and the temperature's dropping fast. Ice is bad on the road."

The next morning dawned clear, but a wind from the northwest had brought bitter cold air down from Canada. It was only four above zero when Don ran out to look at the thermometer. After breakfast he dressed in his warmest clothes and went down to the dock. Ice lay thick all along the marshy edge of the bay—a sight he had rarely seen— there in the salt water.

He stayed only a moment, but before he got back to the house, his ears were numb with cold, and he had to rub them hard to bring back the circulation. He was sure now that they would have no visit from Cameron. But he was wrong.

About eleven o'clock the horn of the Volkswagen beeped in the dooryard. "Ahoy the house!" Alec called cheerfully, and came tramping into the kitchen. He was dressed in a fur-lined parka and thick wool gloves, and the cold didn't seem to bother him.

"Did you get my letter?" he asked. "What did you think of the Hester Winters story?"

Don told him he thought it sounded a bit fishy, and why. Then he went on to describe what he had found down near the big cedar.

"No way to be sure," he said, "but it looked as if somebody had dug some holes and then filled them in again pretty carefully."

Cameron nodded as if he had expected some such development. "I'd like to go down there and look around," he said. "Get into the warmest things you own, and we'll take a shovel along."

This time Don put on a knitted skating cap to protect his ears. He brought a shovel from the tool house, and they got into the warm car. At the last minute Bullet came rushing out, and they let him in with them.

"The roads are a bit slick," Cameron said, "but that's one advantage of a rear-engine car. We won't do any skidding."

Twenty minutes later, they had parked below the old cedar and were over the dune. The sand, drenched by the rain and then frozen, was covered by a crust almost as hard as rock. When they reached the area of the digging, Alec nodded. The five spots Don had noticed were still visible as slightly sunken depressions. Alec looked them over and nodded again. He paced from one to the next and looked up to estimate the distance from each to the blazed cedar.

"Did you notice," he mused, "that these places lie in a sort of semicircle, and each of them is about the same distance from that tree? Just about a hundred and fifty feet, I'd say. So maybe the tree *does* have something to do with what's going on."

He took the shovel and started to dig into the frozen sand. It was hard going at first. In a dozen attempts he only succeeded in breaking through a small area. Then, below, he found the unfrozen sand much easier to dig. He rested when he had gone down two or three feet, and Don took a hand at it. His leg hampered him, however, and after a few minutes he had to give up.

"I think that's deep enough." Cameron chuckled. "If I'm right, we won't prove anything, anyhow."

He took back the shovel and began carefully separating and sifting the sand they had removed. When he finished, he stood there in thought. "I just wondered if we'd find an old coin or two," he said. "But there's nothing here as you can see."

At that moment, they heard Bullet bark down at the edge of the marsh. Don whistled to him, but he only barked louder.

"Come on," said Cameron. "Let's see what's got him so excited."

Just beyond the dog was a little cove, frozen over. And there in the ice, a few yards from shore, a small duck was struggling. It was a species Don didn't remember seeing, black and white, with a big round head. It flapped its wings frantically but was unable to rise.

"Frozen in!" said Alec. "Here—I'll crawl out there and chop away the ice with the shovel."

He stretched out full length on his stomach and pushed himself along the frozen surface. A few feet from the duck, he lifted the shovel and brought the edge down hard on the ice. It was only an inch thick, and the blow shattered it. Again Cameron struck, this time on the other side of the trapped bird. The duck gave another frenzied flap, and the ice broke loose from its feet, tinkling down in pieces. In an instant, the frightened creature was flying off across the bay.

"Gosh!" said Don. "You sure knew how to do that! What kind of a duck was it?"

"A little bufflehead," Alec panted. "They don't usually winter here. I imagine he was with a flock headed south. Probably went to sleep and waited too long to take off when the freeze started."

"Well," Don said with a grin, "it was tough luck on him, but he did get away, thanks to you. Anyhow, he makes my forty-eighth bird!"

As they turned back toward the dune, Bullet raced on ahead of them.

"Look at that fool dog!" Don cried. "He's digging the rest of the hole you started."

The big retriever was nearly out of sight in the excavation, throwing out sand furiously.

"Acts as if he thought there was a bone down there." Don chuckled.

But a moment later, neither of them was laughing. Bullet emerged holding something gently in his mouth and brought it to his master. When he laid it down, they stared in horror. It was the skeleton of a human hand.

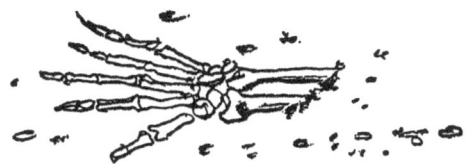

The white bones, no longer firmly joined together, fell in a loose pile as soon as they were dropped, but there was no question about what they were. Cameron stooped over and picked up one of the larger bones gingerly. He tapped it against his other hand, then blew on it to remove some of the loose sand. With his pocket microscope, he examined first one end, then the other. Then, to Don's astonishment, he smiled.

"Here," he said, "let's put this back where it came from

and fill in the hole. I don't aim to do any more digging today, but I'd be willing to wager that each of these five spots would have other bones in it—maybe a skull or a spine or a human thigh bone. Tell me, what did you think when you saw what Bullet had dug up?"

"Why," Don stammered, "I guess I thought of that poor seaman that Captain Kidd buried on top of the treasure chest."

Cameron nodded. "Exactly," he said. "That's what you—or somebody else—were supposed to think. But I'll tell you a secret. I know now that this whole thing is a clever fake. Don't tell anybody I said so because I'd like to give the tricksters more rope and let them hang themselves."

He picked up the small bones with care, carried them to the pit, and laid them in the bottom. Then, with the shovel, he scooped the sand back in, tamped it, and leveled it.

"Come on," he said with a shiver, "let's head back to your place. It's just too cold to stay around here."

THIRTEEN

Don was still somewhat bewildered as they drove homeward. His own first impulse, when Bullet turned up the bones, was to grab the shovel and go after the treasure. But apparently Cameron was sure they would have found no chest of gold if they had dug the hole deeper. Though the scientist had said nothing more, it was obvious that something about the bone he had examined made him positive he had uncovered an elaborate hoax. Naturally Don was disappointed, but he was ready to heed his friend's warning and say nothing about it.

Cameron stayed to lunch with the family and talked gaily of the cold and of the bufflehead duck they had liberated from the ice. Then he told them he had written to the famous Mariners Museum in Virginia about the figurehead of the *Clara May.*

"They have a number of fine figureheads," he said. "I've been down there and seen them, but I doubt if any are handsomer than yours. The museum can't afford to spend much money for such things, but if they're interested, I expect you'll get something for it."

Don went out to the car with him when he left. "Remember, now," said Alec, "don't say anything about what we found. Before very long, I have a hunch you'll see all the pieces of your puzzle fall into place. So long, now!"

For the next few weeks, Don watched hopefully for a letter with a Virginia postmark. He had decided that if the Mariners Museum showed any interest in his figurehead, he would be glad to let them have it for nothing. It would be an honor to know it stood among other relics of the sea where thousands could admire it.

The weather moderated in the week after Cameron's visit, and by early February, there came a few days of balmy south wind that made Don almost believe spring was at hand. He certainly didn't want to stay in the house on that fine Saturday. He packed himself a lunch and started hiking south. With a few stops to watch the gulls along the beach, he passed the Coast Guard station and reached the old cedar before noon. There he sat down and ate his sandwiches. The gnarled, twisted trunk rose above him, and he could see the scar on its side, the gray stain now appearing almost natural after the weathering it had taken. When he had rested and finished eating, Don crossed through the fringe of trees and went down the west side of the dune.

He was looking for the five places that had been dug and covered over again. To his surprise, not one of them was to be seen. Somebody had been there since the thaw and had raked the sand smooth again. There were even a few driftwood sticks scattered over the surface to make it look as if it had lain undisturbed for years.

Don remembered the bones of a human hand buried in the hole Alec had dug, and he shuddered. Then something clicked in his mind. Earlier that week there had been an incident in biology class that had meant little to him at the time. The teacher, Mr. Reynolds, had told them the previous Friday that the class would be taking up the study of the structure of the human skeleton on Monday. But when the time came, he had made a change in assignments. "Due to a little difficulty we've had," he said, "we'll start with the muscles first, using these color charts."

None of the pupils had paid much attention to that "little difficulty" he mentioned. Bones—muscles—which group they studied first made little difference to them. But now Don wondered. Had something happened to the school skeleton? It was kept, he had heard, in a locked closet in the biology laboratory. He had never seen it himself, but there were tales about the skeleton once being stolen as a Halloween prank. It was returned the next day, the story went, and as far as Don knew, the guilty boys had never been punished.

Short of asking Mr. Reynolds a direct question, he didn't see how he was to find out if the bones were still there. So all he felt he could do was wait and see what happened. As Alec Cameron had told him, the pieces of the puzzle were starting to fall into place.

That night he wrote to his friend, the professor. "I thought you'd be interested to know," he said, "that the sand diggings have all been smoothed over and a few sticks thrown around to hide them. Also, I'm not certain yet, but I think the high school's skeleton is missing from the biology lab."

On the following Tuesday, the mail brought him two letters. One was an answer from Alec Cameron. It was a brief note thanking him for the information and winding up with the cryptic statement that "things are beginning to break at this end, too."

What he meant Don could only guess, but it gave him a feeling of confidence. Evidently Cameron had started his own investigation of the mystery of the marked tree and the human bones.

The other envelope bore a New York postmark, and his name and address were crudely printed with a pencil in capital letters. It looked as if a child had sent it. Frowning, he opened the envelope and found a note on cheap, ruled paper.

"IF YOU WANT TO STAY HEALTHY," it said, "YOU'LL KEEP AWAY FROM A CERTAIN PART OF THE ISLAND AND KEEP YOUR MOUTH SHUT. YOU KNOW WHAT I'M TALKING ABOUT."

There was no signature. Don read it over a second time and felt a chill run down his spine. He had never before received a threatening letter. Except for the postmark, he would have suspected it was written by young Jimson. But what would Digger be doing in New York? Besides, he had seen the boy in school that day, and there had been no more than the usual teasing remarks—no special glare of hatred and no spoken threats.

Don had said nothing to his father about the hand bones he and Alec had found, and he hesitated to speak to him now. But sooner or later, the superintendent would be involved. Perhaps he had better show him the note.

At that moment a car drove up to the house, and he heard John Douglas's hearty voice talking to some other person. Quickly he slipped both letters into his pocket just as the door opened.

"Glad you're home from school, Don," said his father. "Here's a gentleman wants to talk to you."

With the menacing note still uppermost in his mind, Don gave the visitor a hurried glance. He certainly didn't look like a gunman. He was short, stooped, gray-haired and wore thick glasses.

"This is Mr. Malcolm, Don," his father went on. "He's driven all the way up here from Virginia to have a look at the figurehead of the *Clara May*."

"Gosh, Mr. Malcolm," Don stammered in relief, "that's a long trip! I guess you must be tired."

"It didn't take so long," the elderly man replied with a

twinkle. "The Chesapeake bridge-tunnel and the Cape May ferry make it easy nowadays. I won't drive back till tomorrow, but meanwhile I'm anxious to see this discovery of yours."

It was still daylight, and Don led the way to the tool shed and flung open the door. There stood the old carving with its worn but handsome woman's face.

Mr. Malcolm peered at it from various angles. "Lovely!" he murmured. "A real find. For years I've been hoping to get a genuine Elijah Kittredge figurehead, and apparently there's no doubt about the authenticity of this one."

He got down on his knees for a closer examination of the base of the carving. "E. K. '85," he said. "I've checked on the wreck of the *Clara May*, and it all fits. It was a lucky day for the museum when you found this, my boy!"

"Do you plan to take her back with you?" asked Don a bit wistfully.

"Why, yes, if we can come to terms. I'm prepared to offer you a hundred dollars. Wish it could be more, but our funds are limited. I came up in a panel truck, as you can see, so there's no problem about carrying the lady."

"What do you say, son?" asked John Douglas. "The price sounds fair enough to me."

"Yes, sir!" Don replied. "A hundred dollars'll be fine. And some day I hope we can go down to Newport News and see all the things you've got there."

The man beamed. "I'm sure you'd like it," he said. "Our exhibits are unique, with everything from early log canoes to scale models of great liners. There are relics from warships of all kinds, too."

He gave Don a check forthwith, and at Mrs. Douglas's insistence, he spent the night with them. All through the evening there was good talk about ships and shipwrecks, for Mr. Malcolm knew his maritime history intimately. He had lived with things that had been saved from the vessels themselves.

It wasn't until the next afternoon that Don had an opportunity to show his father the anonymous letter. At first John Douglas was inclined to think little of it, suggesting that some boy at school was playing a prank on him. But when Don told him the rest of the story and described the skeleton of a hand that Bullet had dug up, he grew more serious.

"I think perhaps you'd better stay clear o' that place down the island," he said. "It just might be they mean it. Meanwhile, we'll keep a close watch on everybody that comes through the gates, and I'll do a bit of patrolling in the boat. I don't like to call in the State Police until we have more to go on."

Several weeks went by with no further developments, and Don began to think nothing was going to happen after all. His father had gone out at dusk in the motorboat a number of times but had seen no suspicious craft and no activity along the shore.

Spring was in the wind on the second Saturday in March, and Don needed exercise. He hiked down the island as far as the Coast Guard station, hoping he might find his friend Tom Coleman and ask if he had noticed anything happening farther down.

The breeze was westerly, and to his delight it brought him the song of redwing blackbirds from the marsh. They were among the first birds to return—a sure sign of coming spring, the old baymen said. A few minutes later, he heard the lilt of a song sparrow in the bayberry clumps. It was early for song sparrows to come back, but there was no mistaking that musical call. It wouldn't be long now, he thought, before the migratory water birds would be arriving.

A mile or so above the station, there was an area of low dunes, bare of trees and covered only by waving beach grass. As he passed, a flutter of white wings caught his attention. Sure that it wasn't a herring gull he had seen, he clambered up through the sand—and was suddenly attacked by a pair of terns. They screamed at him in rage and darted at his head, swerving off at the last second. Don ducked and laughed. It was too early, he knew, to find a nest with any eggs, but the terns were obviously preparing for the mating season. They would scoop out a shallow hole in the sand, and when the time came, the female would lay her eggs there. He didn't want to discourage them, so he beat a retreat to the road and went on his way.

As he neared the station, he saw a Coast Guard jeep approaching in the distance. Just before it turned in, Tom Coleman, who was at the wheel, recognized him and stopped till he came up.

When they had exchanged greetings, Don asked the young seaman if he had seen any more night prowlers on his patrol.

"Can't say I have," Coleman replied. "Far's I can tell, it's all quiet down there. I did see a boat, though. It was around dusk a few nights ago. She was about a twenty-footer, an' she was movin' slow, without lights, pretty well inshore. I looked again on the way back, but by that time she'd gone."

"Are you sure it wasn't my dad's boat?" asked Don. "He's been keeping an eye on the shore down here."

"Nope," Coleman replied with certainty. "This was a sort of a small cruiser—inboard engine an' a decked cabin. Not one o' the boats Jimson rents for fishin', either. What do you say—you want a lift home, or are you goin' on down to the big cedar?"

Don shook his head. "I'm turning back here," he said, "but I'll hike it. Thanks for the offer, but I need to walk."

On the way home, he wondered about the boat Tom had seen. There was nothing unusual about motorcraft moving up and down the bay, for it was part of the Intracoastal Waterway. However, the buoyed channel was some distance from the island.

Later, as Don was nearing the house, a sporty-looking Jaguar convertible came purring down the road. The top was down, and he saw there was only one man in the car—a tight-lipped fellow, wearing a tweed jacket and a black beret. He gave Don a hard look as he spun past.

Don watched the car till it disappeared around a slight curve, far down the island. Then he went on past the house and approached the guard at the gate.

"Hi, Eddy," he said. "Pretty nice sports car that was that just came through. What kind of a guy was he? Didn't look like a surf fisherman to me."

"No." Eddy chuckled. "I'd have said he was some sort of a big-shot gangster type if he hadn't been wearing them fancy clothes. He said he was interested in our wildlife. Here's his name in the book—Mr. A. Varano—and his address is somewhere in the Bay Ridge section of Brooklyn."

Don returned home worrying about Mr. A. Varano. Was he connected in any way with Blake and Fallon, or whatever their real names were? It struck him that Eddy's description was a good one. If he had seen the man's face in a movie, he would have taken him for a big-time hoodlum, and the sports jacket and beret looked out of place on him.

He kept an eye on the front window the rest of the day, for he wanted to know how much time the nature lover in the Jaguar would spend at the lower end of the island. It was nearly five o'clock when he saw the convertible speeding northward. From that distance it was impossible to see the driver's face clearly, but he seemed to be in a hurry. The low-slung car must have been going better than sixty miles an hour before it came to a screaming stop at the gate.

Early that evening there was a phone call for Don. It was Alec Cameron, and he sounded gay and excited.

"I've got some news for you," he said, "but it can wait till I come down there. If all goes well, I'll be driving down two weeks from today. Anything happening on the island?"

"Not much," Don answered. "But there was a man named Varano in a Jag here today." He described the man's looks and dress and said he had spent at least four hours down the island.

"Varano, eh?" said Alec. "That's interesting. There's a Tony Varano who's pretty high up in the New York rackets. Was his first name Antonio?"

"He just signed the book, 'A. Varano,' " Don told him.

"Well, well!" Cameron chuckled. "The wolf trapped by the fox! That's a good one!"

"What—what do you mean?" asked Don, completely befuddled.

"I'll explain when I see you," Alec said. "Got to run now."

And with that he hung up, leaving his young friend more in the dark than ever.

FOURTEEN

Some time in the night, Don woke and lay in the dark, listening. The sound that had wakened him had stopped for a moment, but now it came again, like the faraway yelping of a pack of beagles on a hot trail. A flock of geese was flying over—the big, beautiful Canada geese he had seen in the fall. There must have been a lot of them, for their voices continued minute after minute as they streamed northward across the night sky. He snuggled under the covers, and his heart beat faster at the sound. Spring was really on the way.

He speculated about the "news" Alec Cameron said he would have for them. It was going to be hard waiting two weeks before he heard it. But guessing what it might be got him nowhere, and he finally fell asleep once more.

At school that week, a long wooden box was delivered to the biology laboratory, and Don watched Garry Reynolds open it one afternoon after school when the bus was late. As he had half expected, it contained a skeleton. This one, however, was made of plastic instead of real human bones. He yearned to ask the teacher what had happened to the old skeleton but managed to keep quiet.

"There," said Reynolds in pleased tones, "now we can study bone structure, as we should have earlier."

Don shot a glance at Digger Jimson the next day when the plastic skeleton was set up in the classroom, but the boy appeared unperturbed. After all, if he had any part in stealing the former one, he was probably relieved to see that the school had given up trying to recover it.

In the middle of the last week in March, there came a day or two of warm, balmy weather following rain, and the grass in the Douglases' dooryard suddenly showed a tinge of new green. Now Don was sure that spring was at hand. He polished the lenses of his binoculars and prepared to find more birds for his list. However, the wind shifted into the northeast, and by Thursday evening it had turned cold again.

Don was walking north to catch the school bus Friday morning when he heard a horn sound behind him. A jeep pulled up alongside, and there was Tom Coleman at the wheel.

"Thought I'd catch you about this time," said the Coast Guardsman with a grin. "I wanted to tell you I saw lights again near the big cedar last night. I went to the top o' the dune for a look, but it was all dark again by that time. Reckon they must ha' heard the car stop an' hid themselves. Anyhow, I figured you'd want to know."

Don thanked him and went on across the bridge. The news was just what he had been expecting, but he wasn't quite sure what to do about it. However, it appeared that whatever was going on in the area behind the old tree was now happening at night. Surely, he thought, he wouldn't be running any risk if he took a look at the place in the daytime.

School was dismissed early that last Friday before spring vacation, and Don was at home by three. Hurriedly he put on old clothes, told his mother he was going for a hike, and set off down the road. The weather was still chilly and partly cloudy. He was glad of the warmth of the old mackinaw he wore.

Walking steadily, he passed the Coast Guard station well before five and hastened on while the sun still peeped through the clouds in the west. There was an hour or so of daylight left when he reached the big cedar tree.

Before he climbed into the woods, Don stopped and listened. But the only sound that reached him was the mewing of the gulls on the beach. He went on cautiously to the foot of the blazed tree. Around it, the sand seemed to be disturbed, as if someone had walked there, but he couldn't be sure.

The eerie stillness of the place made him jumpy. Careful to stay hidden, he moved on through the trees and peered down the slope of the dune. Fifty yards away, where the signs of digging had been, he saw a pile of sand and beside it what looked like a deep hole. He crouched and watched, holding his breath, but nothing moved down there. Finally curiosity got the better of him. Gathering his courage, he went down the hill, his eyes fixed on the sand heap.

As he came nearer, he saw a shovel lying beside the hole and hesitated before going on. The quiet reassured him. Quickly now he went the rest of the way at his hopping run and knelt down to look into the hole. It was some five or six feet deep. The sand looked damp and freshly dug. And there at the bottom he saw a grinning skull and a gleam of coins. He leaned still lower for a closer inspection just as a faint

sound came from behind him. Before he could move, there was a sudden blow on the back of his head, and blackness engulfed him.

*　　*　　*

The first thing Don was conscious of, when he came to, was the painful throbbing in his skull, made worse by the roar of an engine. There was a fishy smell of bilge and oil around him, and he was aware of motion—the jarring heave of a boat being driven at full speed.

He groaned and tried to sit up but found his wrists tied behind him and his ankles also bound. Opening his eyes, he could see the dirty green planking of a cockpit and two men hunched on the after thwart. The one who was steering at the outboard tiller was small and red-haired, with a foxy, sharp-nosed face. The other, bigger and darker, he recognized as the man called Blake. Don lay still then and waited for the pounding in his head to cease. Bitterly he blamed himself for what was happening to him. That note he had received should have warned him, but after weeks had gone by, he had grown cocky about it. Now, he realized with a sinking heart, his life was really in danger.

"Put a blindfold on him," came a sharp order from the helmsman. And the big man stooped beside Don and tied a dirty rag around his eyes.

"He's awake," Blake's gruff voice announced. "Want me to sock him again?"

"No," Fallon answered. "If he can walk, we won't have to lug him."

The boat continued to pound along, and Don, unable to see now, tried to figure where it was headed. They were still in the bay, he was sure, for the waves were short and choppy and there was no ocean swell. But how far had they come?

He heard Fallon cut the motor, and the boat lost way, drifting through marsh grass that scraped along the gunwale. Then the bow plowed into something that felt like mud.

"O.K.," said Fallon. "Haul him out an' get him up to the shack. He'll be safe enough there. But unless you want to carry the punk, you'd better get that rope off his legs."

Blake growled something under his breath and worked at the knot that held the boy's ankles. Then he jerked him roughly to his feet and over the boat's side. Don felt his shoes sink into soft muck. With Blake shoving him from behind, he stumbled through the reeds to higher ground.

It took them perhaps ten minutes of walking to reach the shack Fallon had mentioned. Don was pushed through a doorway, where he tripped over the rotting sill and fell headlong on a floor made of splintery boards.

"Seems like it would ha' been less trouble to bury him in the hole," the bigger man grumbled.

"Shut up!" snapped Fallon. "For your part o' ten grand, you'll do as I say. Maybe it'll be twenty grand by this time tomorrow. I think I've got another sucker hooked. All right, tie up his legs again and let's get out o' here. Don't worry about the kid. Just leave him like he is, an' he won't move an inch. Maybe we'll even be back here in the morning."

He heard the pair go out, then the receding tramp of their feet on the marshy ground. After a while there was the sound of the outboard starting up. As soon as he was sure they were gone, Don turned on his back and began rubbing the knot of the blindfold against the floor. A minute or two of this painful exercise loosened the rag, and he was able to see again.

Through the open door, the eastern sky was growing dark. It must be well past six o'clock, he judged, and the sun had set. Inside the cabin there was little to see. There was no furniture of any kind. In a corner lay a rumpled old blanket, and nearer to his side was a dirty glass jug, half full of water. He was thirsty, but tied up as he was, getting at the water was impossible.

Somehow, while there was still daylight, he had to untie the rope that chafed his wrists. But no matter how hard he tried, he couldn't get a finger into the knot. At last, bruised and bleeding and bone-tired, he gave it up.

For a while Don lay there panting, fighting back the tears. Then he grew angry at himself. He had been through other troubles without quitting, and he thought that a boy who had come back from the paralysis of polio ought to have courage enough to get out of this jam. He rolled over, feeling for a knife, a tin can, even a loose nail in the floorboards. When it became apparent that there was simply nothing there, he made himself as comfortable as he could, lying on his side, and resolved to get some sleep.

That was more easily said than done. He worried about what his family would think when he didn't come home. As far as he knew, nobody had seen him from the time he left the house, and of course, he hadn't told his mother where he meant to go. There were noises in the dark, too, that kept him from sleeping. Some animal went past through the grass —probably a muskrat, he thought. Then a night heron uttered its guttural *quawk*, and somewhere in the distance, he heard the mournful hooting of an owl. In the stillness that followed, there was no sound of cars. Wherever the shack stood, it must be a long way from any road.

It was while he lay puzzling over its location that he drifted off into a troubled slumber. When he woke with the first beam of sun in his eyes, his first thought was that he was half frozen. Then he remembered where he was and went through a few bad moments, but his courage came back quickly. He sat up, groaning at the stiffness in his joints, and went to work on the knots once more.

Now, at last, he had a bit of luck. Close to the wall of the shack, beneath what had been a window, the sun glinted on a piece of glass! Don worked his way over to it and found several scraps of the broken pane. He chose one that seemed to have a particularly sharp edge, got a grip on it with his right hand, and began sawing at the rope. It was awkward to handle behind his back. Twice his fingers slipped, and he

knicked the skin of his wrist. But finally he could feel the strands of hemp begin to fray. After what seemed a long time, the rope fell away, and he brought his arms painfully forward.

It took a few minutes to work the feeling back into his numb fingers. His wrists were badly chafed, but most of the bleeding had stopped. Untying the rope around his ankles came more easily now, and soon he was free—able to stand up and to walk!

He limped to the door and looked around. It was a fine, bright morning with redwing blackbirds singing loudly on the marsh. Barely a quarter of a mile eastward was the bay, and beyond it the line of Topsail Island. He could make out the lookout tower on the Coast Guard station and farther south the dark mass of trees near the old cedar.

Don's mouth was very dry. He pulled the stopper out of the jug, sniffed at the water, and had a long drink. Then he went out behind the shack to look toward the mainland. It seemed even farther away than the island, for the marsh was very wide here and interlaced with tidal creeks. It would take hours of walking and probably some swimming to reach it.

An hour later there came the drone of an engine in the sky, and he turned eastward again to see a small plane cruising above the bay. His heart gave a jump. That was the Coast Guard amphibian! Was it possible they were already out searching for him? He waved his arms wildly, though he knew it was hopeless, for the plane was a good two miles away.

The little aircraft held its course up the bay, but before it disappeared, Don saw two good-sized motorboats moving southward at slow speed. One, he was sure, was his father's. Hastily he looked around for some means of signaling, and his eye fell on the broken glass under the window. There was one piece nearly four inches across, and when he had poured a little water on it and rubbed it with the blanket, it gleamed brightly.

Rushing outside with the glass in his hand, Don held it so that the sun's rays caught it and sent a reflected beam eastward over the bay. It was impossible to put the light exactly where he wanted it because of the distance, but he kept trying, flashing the beam on and off. The two searching craft held the same steady pace and were soon far down the bay.

In desperation, Don ran back to the shack. He thought he remembered seeing something else in the pile of trash under the window. Feverishly he fumbled through the bits of glass and dirt till he found what he wanted. It was an old match folder with two paper matches left in it. Now he needed something to burn. Outside he grabbed handfuls of marsh grass and broken twigs from a withered bush. Carefully he made a loose pile of the tinder, and then, with trembling fingers, he scratched a match. It sizzled and went out.

This would be his last chance, and Don drew a long breath to steady himself before he tried again. The match flared, and he sheltered it with a cupped hand, holding the flame close to the brown grass. After an anxious moment it caught!

Hastily he brought more grass and more twigs—greener now. A cloud of dense, dark smoke went up as he added them to the fire.

FIFTEEN

As soon as he was sure his smudge was working, Don brought the old blanket from the cabin. Never in his life had he tried to make smoke signals, but he had to try now. He remembered the SOS code—three short, three long, three short—and made an attempt to reproduce it with smoke. The first time he covered the fire with the blanket, it nearly went out. Only by frantic blowing and adding more dry grass did he bring the sparks back to life. He saw he would have to get a good hot bed of coals before he could make any signals.

So, for half an hour, he gathered more sticks and fed them to the blaze. Meanwhile, he kept glancing toward the bay, fearing every moment he might see his captors coming back. There were several reasons why he had been afraid to cross the marsh when he first got free. First, he would have no cover and would be in plain sight all the way. Second, he knew nothing about the mainland shore in that area. And finally, there were the many creeks to cross, and the water was still icy cold. Yet, as time passed, he began to think he would have to make the effort.

When the fire was at last strong enough to serve his purpose, he threw on another armful of greener hay and prepared to use the blanket once more. The trouble was that by now there were no boats in sight, no plane in the sky.

Don let the dark cloud of smoke go up without trying to

check it. If there were any eyes to see it, he knew it could be seen. Meanwhile, he prayed silently that his kidnapers were still far away.

Looking up the bay, he saw a speck in the sky that must be the Coast Guard search plane returning. He tossed the blanket over the fire, lifted it long enough to let a short burst of smoke escape, and repeated the operation to spell out three "dots." After a longer interval, he jerked off the blanket again, to make the first of the three "dashes." But less and less smoke was now rising, and the center of the blanket was almost charred through.

He raced to throw on more green hay, then doused the burning cloth with water from the jug. His timing was off, however, and by the time he tried to put up a second long smoke, the fire seemed to be dying.

The plane flew past serenely, still far to the east. Panting and discouraged, Don flung himself down. Now, he thought dismally, there was nothing left but to try to cross the marsh. Wearily he got to his feet, but before he set out through the muck, he took one last look at the bay.

There was something coming up from the southeast—a boat—not an outboard but a bigger boat, moving fast, with spray flying from her bows! He stood staring, wondering why she was headed straight toward the shack. And then he saw that the fire he thought was dead was throwing up a spiral of smoke once more.

As the boat came closer, he knew it was his father's. His effort to send signals had saved him after all. Hurrying toward the shore of the bay, Don stood there waving his arms till he was sure the occupants of the boat had seen him.

John Douglas was at the wheel. He reduced speed and

brought his craft slowly in till the bow scraped mud. Standing amidships was Alec Cameron, and as soon as the keel touched, he sprang overboard to wade ashore. Both men were serious-faced.

"Are you all right, Don?" called the professor. "You had us scared. Come on and get in. You can tell us how you got here on the way home."

They doused the fire and stamped it out. As Don clambered over the boat's side, his father put an arm around his shoulders. "Hey!" he exclaimed. "What happened to your wrists?"

"They tied me up with ropes," Don told him. "I had to cut myself loose with a piece o' broken glass."

Both men stared at him, open-mouthed. "*Who* tied you up?" asked his father. "You mean you didn't come over here by yourself?"

" 'Course not. I didn't have a boat. It was those two—Blake and Fallon. They'd dug a hole that looked like a grave, six feet long and a couple o' feet wide. It was deep, too. I guess they hid behind the pile o' sand when I went down there for a look. I bent down over the hole and saw a skull and some silver money, and just then they clubbed me on the back o' my head."

His father and Cameron stared at each other. "Go on," said John Douglas with a hard glint in his eye.

"I was out for a while," said Don, "but when I came to, they had me in a boat—one o' Jimsons', I think—and we were headed over here. Blake blindfolded me and dragged me to that shack, and pretty soon they went off again. I guess they figured I was tied up so tight I'd never get out. Did you see the smoke signals I was trying to send?"

Alec Cameron chuckled. "I did," he said. "I was on the

island right where you'd been. There's no hole there now, though. It's all filled in and smoothed over. When I saw the smoke, I called your father and here we are."

Don's father started the engine and backed off the mudbank. "You sure had us mystified," he said. "Of course, we didn't get worried till it was way past suppertime and you hadn't come home. Then I drove down the island and checked with the Coast Guard, but they hadn't seen you. Finally I called the State Police, and they've been hunting for you ever since.

"It wasn't until Alec came this morning that we decided to search the dune below the old cedar. I told him you'd promised to keep away from there, but it was about the only place left."

He looked at Don reproachfully, and the boy hung his head.

"I know, Dad," he mumbled. "I acted like a dumb kid, going there, and I guess I got just what I deserved."

"Never mind—you're safe now, thank goodness. But I'd better get home and call the police."

"Tell me, Don," said Alec as the powerful engine sent them up the bay, "did those two do any talking?"

"Not much. I found out that Fallon gives the orders, though. Blake is just around to do the strong-arm jobs. Fallon told him they already had ten thousand dollars, and he expected to make it twenty by tonight. He said he thought he had 'another sucker hooked.' "

Alec Cameron nodded and looked pleased. "What did I tell you, John?" he said. "Tony Varano was just the first one. Now, if we can keep Don's disappearance out of the news, the second sucker is pretty sure to come on the scene."

"What I want," growled the superintendent, "is to get my hands on the pair that kidnaped my boy!"

"They shouldn't be too hard to trace," Cameron told him. "But don't expect to see them back here for a while. I think they've done their work, salting those fake graves. Now they'll concentrate on selling maps to more pigeons."

Don had only a vague glimmer of what he meant, but he did remember one remark the kidnapers had made.

"I figure they do mean to come back," he told Alec. "Just before they left, Fallon told Blake not to worry about me. He said, 'Maybe we'll even be back here in the morning.' "

"Maybe so," John Douglas put in, "but I doubt if they cared much whether you lived or died. You were just a nuisance to their plans, and all they wanted was to make sure you were out of the way."

They landed at the home dock and went up to the house.

"Don," his father warned him, "get yourself cleaned up before your mother sees you. You're all mud and blood and soot."

He went on in to give the good news to Mrs. Douglas while Alec helped Don wash at the tap in the garage. By the time he was presentable and had been thoroughly hugged by his mother, John Douglas was on the phone, talking to the State Police.

"Safe and sound," Don heard him say. "Remember the two men in the Cadillac that came down here last fall? I asked for a check on the license, and you said it belonged to a fellow named Balichek, from Brooklyn. The names they gave us were Blake and Fallon. Anyhow, they're the ones who knocked out Don and left him tied up in a shack on the marsh over your side o' the bay."

"Wait," Cameron whispered. "Let me talk a second."

When he had the receiver, he introduced himself as a friend of the family. "I think," he said, "you may find the little red-haired man called Fallon has an alias, too. He may be posing as some kind of archeologist and calling himself Mr. Kurt Falkenhein. One thing I'm pretty sure of is that he's an expert forger and confidence man—probably with a police record. Right now he's trying to sell treasure maps to hand-picked prospects with lots of ready money."

He answered a few questions and hung up. Then he turned to the Douglases with a comical expression on his face.

"Great heavens!" he exclaimed. "In all the excitement I forgot the news I'd come here to tell you! As soon as school and college are out this June, Amanda Carter and I are getting married!"

Don's jaw dropped. All he could do was stare at his friend and whisper, "Gosh!"

"I know what you're thinking," Alec said with a laugh. "You're going to lose your favorite teacher at school. But I promise we'll come to see you all here."

"Well," said Mrs. Douglas, beaming, "I, for one, am not surprised, and it couldn't happen to two nicer people!"

When the congratulations were over, Don returned to the subject of the two kidnapers. "I'd wondered about that man Falkenhein, too," he said. "Wouldn't the reporter on the New York tabloid be able to identify him? I mean the one that dug up the note to Hester Winters in the attic of that old house?"

"Sure, he could," Alec replied. "I tried that, but he wouldn't talk. Claimed it was privileged information of a kind the press doesn't have to disclose. If the police get into this, though, I expect they'll make him sing a different tune."

"Do you figure there'll be more treasure hunters coming to the island?" John Douglas asked. "I was wondering if I'd better ask for more guards."

"I doubt if that's necessary," Cameron told him. "If my

theory's right, you won't see any swarms of diggers coming here. Just two or three, and they'll arrive in secret, one at a time. Tony Varano was probably the first to fall for the treasure map. He has plenty of loose money, itching to be spent, and he's the greedy type. I have a hunch he'd give ten thousand in a minute if he thought it might get him half a million in gold and jewels. His first trip here was just to look over the layout, I expect. When he comes back, he'll be all set to dig, but he won't bring any helpers to share in the treasure. Whatever you do, don't try to stop him. He's a lot too handy with a gun. Just call the State Police and leave it to them."

Shortly after that, he said he had to go, and Don went out to the car with him.

"Gee," the boy told him, "I sure am happy about you and Miss Carter! I hope you can come down before the wedding, though, and help me spot some more birds. They'll be coming north pretty soon, now."

"Things are going to be very busy for me these next two months," Cameron answered with a chuckle. "But if I can make it, I'll be here. Maybe I can persuade Amanda to come with me!"

Don expected trouble in getting to sleep that night. But in spite of all the thoughts whirling through his brain, fatigue caught up with him as soon as his head hit the pillow.

His mother was sure he was in no shape to go to church the next morning. He was clean enough, after a thorough soaping in the shower, but the welt on his head was still swollen, and his chafed wrists looked worse than they felt. So he was left alone on a fine bright spring day. Shortly after the family drove off, he took his field glasses and headed for the beach.

There was no need to go very far south to see birds along

the sands. The familiar sandpipers and sanderlings were there, as well as laughing gulls by the score. They were noisy things but handsome, with their black hoods, and he was glad to see them back. He sighted ringed plovers and ruddy turnstones, as well. Then, at a distance, some larger beach birds came into view through the binoculars. They looked almost exactly like the black-bellied plovers he had spotted in the fall, but as he moved closer, he could see a difference in the color of the back feathers. These had a yellowish russet tinge, instead of being black and white. Beyond any question these were golden plover—a new species for his list!

When he realized that the total had now reached forty-nine, he was fired with ambition to round out the figure. Fifty birds would be more than he had dared to dream of at the start.

On down the beach he went, watching eagerly for new species, but all he found were more of the familiar ones. After a mile or more, he decided to cross over to the bay side of the island. On the marsh he knew there were birds that never came near the beach.

At that point the uneven shore of the bay thrust out in a broad strip of marshland beyond the dunes. He made his way past patches of bayberry and juniper, careful not to step on any terns' nests. They must be there, for numbers of the graceful birds screamed and dived at him as he crossed the dune.

Soon he was down at the edge of a little creek, with bulrushes and marsh grass all around him. An old log, washed in by some forgotten high tide, lay there invitingly. Glad of a chance to rest, he sat down on it and waited, sweeping the nearby marsh with his glasses. There were no egrets yet, for they rarely put in an appearance before the middle of April.

But he did see the dark plumage of little blue herons. And nearer to him, standing so still he didn't spot it at first, was a big grayish bird with a long spear of a beak—his old friend, the great blue heron.

Far off down the bay channel, a fishing boat passed, heading for the inlet at the head of the island. It was a Jersey bank-skiff, built on the general lines of a big dory, with an engine amidships. Many of the commercial fishermen used such craft to go outside and troll on the ridge, a dozen miles off shore.

He watched it for a while idly, then caught a glimpse of movement on the marsh, a hundred yards away. It was another long-legged wading bird that looked almost black from where Don sat. His first guess was that it must be another little blue heron. Then, with the binoculars carefully focused, he saw that the beak was not straight. It had a definite downward curve. And the breast feathers seemed to have a reddish or purplish sheen. He had studied his bird book long enough to know those signs, and he knew he was looking at his first glossy ibis—a rare sight in this latitude!

SIXTEEN

Don watched the dark, graceful wader for another minute to make absolutely sure. Through the glasses he could make out a patch of blue-white between the eyes and the greenish drooping bill. No heron was marked that way. It was indeed a glossy ibis, and he threw his cap in the air to celebrate finding his fiftieth bird!

This was news he felt he had to pass on in a note to Alec Cameron. At once he started back toward the road as fast as his limp would let him. He crossed over the dune and hurried north. Then, as he passed a low place in the dune, half a mile from home, he saw another boat out in the bay. This one was much closer to shore, and it was no bank-skiff but a small, streamlined mahogany runabout. Don stopped and lifted the binoculars for a better look.

In the summer season, there were always boats passing on the Intracoastal Waterway, but they were usually cabin cruisers, much larger than this one. The odd thing about the craft he was watching was its slow speed. Built to do forty miles an hour, it appeared to be creeping along at less than ten. He sharpened the focus and brought the glasses to bear on a lone man at the wheel. Wasn't there something familiar about the set of the sports jacket and the rakish tilt of the beret on his head? With a start, Don knew this was the man he had seen in the Jaguar convertible—the New York gangster known as Tony Varano!

"Golly!" he said in a whisper. And at a hopping run, he went on toward the house. The family car, coming home from church, was just turning in as he reached the driveway, and he hailed his father.

"It's Varano!" he panted. "I just saw him in a motorboat, heading down along the shore o' the island!"

"You're sure?" John Douglas asked with a frown. "How far out was he?"

"Pretty close in and moving slow. It's Varano, all right."

His father still seemed to doubt that Don could have identified a man at that distance.

"Look, Dad," the boy urged. "He had on the same tweed jacket and little black cap. He's headed for that treasure place as sure as anything!"

"Very well," the superintendent agreed as he made up his mind. "I'll call Lieutenant Akins at the State Police barracks."

Don went with him to the office and stood near enough to hear both ends of the conversation. The connection was quickly made.

"Lieutenant?" said Don's father. "This is John Douglas."

"Yes, John—thought I knew your voice. What can I do for you?"

"Remember your talk yesterday with Professor Cameron? One of the people he mentioned to you was an underworld character named Varano. Right? Well, my son is pretty sure he spotted him a few minutes ago. He was in a speedboat, moving south along the shore as if he was looking for a place to land."

There was a moment's pause before Akins replied. "Let's see," he said. "Our nearest police boat is out on patrol, a long way north of you. I'm afraid it would take too long to get there. But I can reach you by car in twenty minutes. O.K.?"

"Good!" John Douglas told him. "We'll be looking for you here."

He hung up and hurried upstairs to change into working clothes. Don was too keyed up to sit still and wait. Though he didn't yet have a driver's license, he knew how to operate a car, so he put the family Buick away and backed out the pick-up truck. Then, in what seemed an incredibly short time, he saw the black-and-white police car come tearing down the road from the gate. The lieutenant must have driven all the way with the accelerator on the floor and the siren screaming.

There was another man in the car with him—a big tanned trooper in uniform. Don's father came out at that moment and greeted the two policemen.

"I'd better lead the way," he said. "There's one particular spot about seven or eight miles south where we think he's headed."

Don was already sitting in the truck. "Hold on, now," his father said. "You ought not to come. Might be some shooting."

"Aw, Dad!" Don pleaded. "I'll stay out o' sight. Besides, I'm the only one that knows Varano when I see him. You're going to need me."

"He's right, John," Akins agreed. "I reckon we can protect him in case any trouble starts."

The superintendent was still doubtful, but he got behind the wheel. He led off, with the police car following, and they drove down the road past the Coast Guard station. As they neared the strip of woods where the big cedar stood, John Douglas held up a warning hand and pulled the truck quietly over on the shoulder, turning off the ignition. Then the four of them moved toward the tree, speaking only in whispers.

Don had visited the place often enough to know where there was good cover. He motioned them up the dune and into the lee of a dense cedar thicket. By crouching below the branches, it was possible to get a view of the sandy area where the bones had been buried. Much to his disappointment, there was nobody there. He whispered as much to his father, who stood cautiously erect and peered through the tops of the young cedars.

"Wait a bit!" the superintendent whispered. "There's a man coming up from the marsh. Must have found a place to beach his boat down there in the cove."

In another moment they could all see him. He picked his way through the salt grass, placing his feet carefully, as if afraid of getting mud on his shiny black shoes. In his hand he was carrying a shovel, brand-new, with the maker's label still on the handle.

They had a good look at him as he came up to the firmer sand at the base of the dune. Once there, he laid down the shovel and pulled a folded paper from his inner jacket pocket. In the stillness they could hear it crackle when he opened it. After a moment of frowning study, he glanced up at the big cedar, then back at what Don was sure must be a map. Then he looked around him at the ground. Three or four paces to his right was a small stick thrust into the sand, and he picked up his shovel and went to the spot.

When he started to dig, Don could hardly hold back a snicker. The man had looked powerful enough in his well-tailored jacket, but apparently he had never done any work with his hands. He was so awkward at digging that it was almost funny.

After half a dozen skimpy shovelfuls had been removed, he paused to rest and mop his forehead with a handkerchief. Then he took off his sports coat and laid it neatly aside. And as he turned, they could see the shoulder holster and the big automatic pistol nestling under his left armpit.

The trooper made an involuntary movement forward, but Akins restrained him, laying a hand on his arm. "Wait," he whispered, "let him work."

Don had been studying the man's face, and there was no question about his being Varano. The gangster kept at his digging until his legs were out of sight in the hole. Finally, when he must have gone down four feet or so, he gave a painful grunt, threw the shovel aside, and sat on the edge of the excavation to catch his breath. There was a look of doubt on his scowling face now.

After a minute, he got up and went to consult the map once more. Then he started up the dune toward the old cedar, taking long, measured strides. Evidently he was pacing off the distance from the hole to the tree.

The lieutenant waited till Varano was less than a dozen yards away, then stepped out into the open.

"Stand where you are," he ordered, "and get your hands high. We've got two guns covering you."

In utter surprise, the gangster whirled to face them, one hand reaching for the automatic. But he found himself staring into the muzzles of the police revolvers, and hastily he put both arms above his head.

"Hey," he snarled, "what is this? You cops got nothin' on me!"

"Only damaging state property and carrying a concealed weapon," Akins told him calmly. "Get his gun, Johnson, and put the cuffs on him."

In a matter of seconds, the man was disarmed and handcuffed.

"Now," said the lieutenant, "you want to tell us what this digging's all about?"

"I ain't tellin' you nothin'," Varano replied sullenly. "Not till I can talk to my lawyer."

"Very well. We'll take you back to headquarters, and you can call him from there. But first we'd better pick up your coat and take a look at that paper you were reading. And what about the boat? You don't want to leave it here, do you?"

"Let it rot, for all I care," growled the gangster.

"I see. That means you don't own it. Better tell us whether it's rented or stolen, so it can be returned."

But Varano balked at giving out that information. He went with them unwillingly to the place where his jacket lay. It was John Douglas who picked it up and removed the map. Don, looking on as he unfolded it, could have believed for a moment that it was genuine. The paper was a yellowed parchment, worn at the edges, and the ink was faded to a pale brown. The chart bore no title—no explanation of what it portrayed. There was simply a crude outline of a long, narrow island. Above it appeared a cross with the points of the compass indicated. A little to the south of the island's middle, a tree was roughly drawn, and beside it, in old-fashioned lettering, the symbols "55 W. by S."

That seemed to be all, except that faintly lettered in one tattered corner Don could read "39° 85′ N.—74° 5′ W." He had no pencil to write the numbers down, but he did his best to memorize them. Once he could get to an atlas, he knew he could verify what he thought they meant. Just then his father noticed the figures, too.

"Well, well," he said. "That's our latitude and longitude right here on Topsail! Or close enough to it to make sure this is the island. Sure looks old, doesn't it?"

Varano was fuming. "O' course it's old!" he snarled.

"More'n two hunnert an' fifty years old. An' it's mine! I paid plenty for it."

"That's right," Akins told him. "Ten grand, wasn't it? They took you for a sucker, Varano. The map's a forgery, and I should think you'd want to get even with the con men who sold it to you. Who are they? Give it to us straight and we won't even book you."

For a second the gangster's face showed astonishment and disgust. Then his mouth set in a hard line, and he shook his head.

"I don't trust no coppers," he said. "Find 'em yourself. There's no rap you can hang on me, anyhow."

"No?" asked the lieutenant. "We could try a charge of stealing a boat for a starter—let alone packing a gun. Might

be a good idea if you'd tell us where you got the boat so we can take it back for you."

Varano had lost some of his bluster now. "Lecky's boat yard," he mumbled. "It's up near Bay Head. I left my car there, too."

"Took quite a trip, didn't you?"

"Sure. I didn't want to come down by road. They ask too many questions at the gate."

"All right," Akins told him. "I'll have the police boat come down here and pick it up. They can fill in the hole you dug at the same time. Let's go."

They marched their prisoner back to the road, got into the cars again, and drove north to the head of the island. There the Douglases drove into their yard, and the police car went on across the bridge.

"What do you think they'll do to him?" Don asked his father.

"Nothing, probably." The superintendent chuckled. "Digging a hole on state property isn't a very serious offense. The concealed weapon charge may let them hold him overnight, but he'll get some slick lawyer to get him off with a small fine. After all, it isn't Varano we want. It's the people who forged the map and took his money. All Akins was trying to do was scare him into giving their names."

"Do you think there'll be more of them coming down here?" Don asked.

"I expect there will. Treasure—big treasure—has a mighty strong pull, and there are always greedy folks who can't resist it. If they come by land, I think our gatemen will be able to spot 'em."

"Yes, but what if they come in boats, like Varano?"

"I've thought about that. Maybe I'll have to post a guard down there after all."

"Gee, Dad!" Don exclaimed. "Could I do it? This next week is spring vacation at school, and I won't have any homework. Besides, I know the place and the best cover to hide in."

His father laughed, but he didn't refuse. "We'll see," was all he would say.

That night as he lay in bed, Don planned it all out. If any treasure hunter came while he was on guard, it would take some time for the measuring and digging. That ought to allow him time to get to the Coast Guard station and telephone his father or the State Police. If only he had a walkie-talkie, everything would be a lot simpler, but there was no chance of that. His first idea would have to work.

He woke early Monday morning and heard a cardinal singing in the first daylight. There weren't many of the handsome red birds on the island, but back of the superintendent's house were some big wild cherry trees, and a pair of cardinals sometimes nested there. The sound reminded Don that more shore birds would be arriving, and there was no reason why he should stop at fifty. Before breakfast he entered the glossy ibis in his book and counted again to make sure he really had that number. Whether he was allowed to stand guard or not, he could take his binoculars to the marsh and try for more new birds.

SEVENTEEN

Breakfast for Don was a leisurely affair that day. His father had to hurry off to work as usual, but with no school, the boy took his time over a second stack of pancakes. Meanwhile, he planned his day. The weather was still fine, and the sun felt almost as warm as May. What he decided to do was take the small outboard boat, which he was allowed to use, and cruise down the bay shore of the island, watching for birds.

He was tempted to take Bullet with him, but the big dog sometimes got restless in a boat, and he might jump overboard if they came close to shore.

Don told his mother what he intended to do and assured her he wouldn't go south of the Coast Guard station. He poured a mixture of gasoline and oil from the red can into the tank and pulled the starter. Once the engine was idling in neutral, he cast off the mooring lines and chugged out into the bay.

There were flocks of birds flying over and settling on the marsh, where low tide had left the mudflats exposed. Many of them looked familiar, but it was hard to identify them without using binoculars, and he was too busy steering to hold the glasses. After twenty minutes or so, he saw a wide stretch of marsh on his left and headed toward it at slow speed. When a tidal creek opened up ahead, he cut the engine and drifted in.

A few birds had taken flight at his approach, but in the silence that followed, they went back to feeding again. Don stood up and slowly and carefully raised his glasses for a closer look. He saw a green heron, a pair of little blue herons, and at a distance a great blue. Most of the birds were smaller, however—sandpipers and plovers, usually seen on the beach. One sandpiper had a different look. Studying it for a moment, he made out a patch of white between the brownish back feathers and the black tail. It was about the size of a sanderling but not so quick in its movements. If his guess was correct, it must be a white-rumped sandpiper.

It was midmorning before he spotted another new bird, and his legs were stiff from standing up in the gently rocking boat. Just as he was about to sit down, a pair of slim grayish birds flew past and lighted on the flats, not a dozen yards away. They had long bills but were smaller than his old friends the willets. And the most prominent feature was the bright yellow color of their legs. They must be lesser yellowlegs.

His hunch about visiting the marsh was paying off. Now he sat down and entered the two new birds in his notebook. It didn't look as if he would get any more, at least in this spot, so he started the motor again and backed out of the creek. Slowly he coasted along the shore till he could see the tower on the Coast Guard station a mile to the south. A cove lay there, close to his port bow, and again he steered in among the tall reeds, switching the engine off as he neared the bank. The only sounds now were the distant piping and whistling of the marsh birds.

Then, startlingly close, came a deep grunting bellow like the voice of a giant bullfrog—*kerlump, kerlump!* Don had heard it before, though he had never caught sight of the bird that made it. Cautiously he stood up in the boat and combed the bulrushes with his binoculars. The sound, when he heard it again, seemed to come from all around him, yet he knew that only one creature was doing the calling.

When the boat's prow bumped the bank, something moved suddenly there in the reeds. It was a chunky brown bird with stiff greenish legs, its long spike of a bill sticking straight upward so that it looked like another bulrush stem.

"American bittern!" Don told himself exultantly. He hoped it would give its croak again, but it had seen him and wanted only to stay hidden. He wished then that he had brought a camera, for at that distance he could have taken a wonderful picture.

Very slowly and quietly, he took an oar and pushed off from the bank, then poled the boat across to the opposite side of the cove. The reeds were lower there, and he would have a better view of the tide flats beyond. Still more flocks of waders were in sight, busily searching the mud for small shellfish and other tidbits.

As Don watched them, his eye caught a different color among the gray, white, and black-and-white birds. One of them was reddish brown with gray wing patches. With the binoculars on it, he could see that it was fairly large, heavier than a willet, and with an even longer bill. Quickly he jotted down a description so that he could find it later in his bird book. One thing was sure—it was a new species to him—his fifty-fourth of the year!

It was pleasant there on the marsh, warm and sunny, but still too early for the mosquitoes that would make life miserable a month or two later. Don watched the birds for another half hour, then started up the motor and headed homeward. As he chugged out of the mouth of the cove, the bittern gave him a farewell salute. *Kerlump, kerlump, kerlump!* It was no wonder, he thought, that old-time baymen called the bird a "thunder-pumper."

It was well before lunchtime when he tied the boat up at the dock. And before doing anything else, he hurried to his room to check the book of water birds. After a bit of searching, he found the color plate that showed the red-brown wader. It was, he found, a dowitcher in spring plumage. When it came back in the autumn, it would be gray—hard to distinguish from some of the others. He wrote down the name with a flourish, along with the white-rumped sandpiper, the lesser yellowlegs, and the American bittern. Fifty-four birds ought to make a list that would attract visitors to Topsail Island!

*　　*　　*

A day of rain and colder weather followed, and Don was glad to stay at home, out of the raw spring winds. He composed a long letter to Alec Cameron, telling about the new birds he had found and then giving the details of Varano's arrest. "Dad called the State Police yesterday," he added, "and they said Varano's lawyer got him out on bail after one night in a cell. He still has to appear in court, though, probably in about a month. We haven't seen any more treasure hunters."

It cleared the next day. After the success he had had in spotting birds from the outboard, Don decided to try it again. He pumped rain water out of the boat and set off shortly after noon. There was a brisk westerly breeze that made the bay choppy. A few wave tops came over the side to splash him, but he had on a waterproof windbreaker and felt no discomfort.

He had been out only ten minutes and was still far north of the Coast Guard tower when another boat passed him, close in. It was a smallish cruiser, white, with mahogany cabin and trim. At the wheel in the cockpit stood a man wearing a huge pale gray ten-gallon hat. He was stocky and broad-shouldered, and when Don put the field glasses on him, he could see a square-jawed, sun-browned face. He looked like a caricature of a Texas millionaire—all except the little cruiser. From his appearance, he should have been the owner of a thousand-ton yacht.

The cruiser was moving fast and throwing up a bow wave that rocked Don's little outboard dangerously.

"You big louse!" the boy exclaimed in anger. But the man in the large hat paid no attention to him or his boat. He churned on, hugging the edge of the marsh and ignoring the channel buoys.

Don watched him out of sight around a point, hoping he would get what he deserved and run the cruiser aground on a mudbank. However, no such disaster happened. Wondering where the man was bound for, Don speeded up. He reached the point opposite the Coast Guard station and looked down the bay, but the cruiser had vanished. That could mean only one thing—the man in the Texas hat had turned into one of the coves.

What was it his father had said? Something about greedy people with a lot of money being the easiest marks for the treasure maps. Perhaps this fellow was the second sucker that Fallon had mentioned! He went on more slowly, scanning the marsh with his glasses, and at last he spied the mahogany cabin among the reeds. It was in almost the same spot where Varano had beached his boat!

Don turned around and headed north, opening up the outboard to top speed. As he flew along, he planned what he should do. His father was over on the mainland and would be away all day, but he knew the possibility of more treasure seekers had been discussed with the guards. If he could get one of them to accompany him, he thought they could handle this new trespasser.

He tied up at the home dock and started for the house at a run. His mother, he was glad to find, was upstairs, and he could call the gate without alarming her.

The man who answered his ring was Matt Cramer, his father's second in command. "Matt," said Don, "could you get away for half an hour? There's a queer duck in a cowboy hat down the island. I'm pretty sure he's landed to look for Captain Kidd's treasure."

Cramer laughed. "Another one?" he asked. "Sure, I'll get one o' the men here to take my place an' meet you in front o' your house in three minutes."

"Good!" said Don. "And maybe you'd better bring a gun."

He could hear the gate guard chuckling. "O.K.," came the answer. "Here I come, loaded for bear."

Don felt relieved. Cramer was an ex-Marine, tough and able. He was almost as quick as he had promised to be. In less than five minutes Don saw the pick-up truck coming down the road from the gate.

"How'd you spot this cowboy character?" Cramer asked as Don got in beside him.

Don explained how he had been out in the boat and seen the cruiser pass. "I don't know how he kept from running aground," he said, "but he steered right into the cove below the old cedar tree."

"Does sound a bit suspicious," the guard replied with a nod. "It won't hurt to ask him a few questions, anyhow."

They drove rapidly southward till they neared the woods where the big cedar stood. Cramer parked the truck a short distance away, and they approached the place on foot.

"The best way," Don whispered, "is to get back o' that cedar thicket an' watch him from there."

He led the way to a good position, screened by the small cedars. They could scan the west slope of the dune and the open sandy area where Don had first discovered the digging.

At first he could see nothing of the stranger. Then he noticed a pile of sand and caught a glimpse of a shovelful flying through the air.

"He's sure down a ways," Cramer whispered admiringly. "There's his big hat over yonder. What do you say? Want to head down there? He won't spot us till we're right on top of him."

Don nodded. "O.K.," he breathed. "Watch out, though. He's probably packing a six-shooter."

He accompanied the guard out into the open, and they moved quickly down the dune. Cramer had loosened the flap of the holster that held his service revolver. As they approached the digging operation, the sand stopped flying. Then a big white string of bones was flung out, and they heard the stranger talking to himself excitedly.

"Feller's backbone, sho' 'nough!" he chortled. "Mus' be that sailor he buried. There's money, too! Three—no four big silver coins. Yessuh, this is it!"

As he started digging furiously once more, Cramer's drawling voice interrupted him. "Don't you know," the guard inquired, "that you're trespassin' on state property?"

The man whirled, dropping his shovel and reaching for the Colt thrust into his belt.

"Now, now," said Cramer, "I wouldn't do that if I was you. Can't you see I've got you covered? Throw your pistol out in the sand, an' come up where we can talk."

The face of the burly stranger was flushed with rage, but after one look into the muzzle of the guard's gun, he obeyed. Clambering out of the pit, he stood there panting and glaring.

"That's better," Cramer told him. "Now let's have your name an' a few other facts. Just in case you're wonderin', I'm a state park guard, with full power to arrest trespassers."

164

The man let out a long breath, and his scowl changed to a grin. "O.K., pardner," he replied. "You've sort o' got the drop on me. Name's Roberts—Austin Roberts. I'm pretty well known in my home state of Oklahoma. Got a big ranch with some cattle, but mostly oil nowadays. As for what I'm doin' here, I was in New York seein' the sights an' spendin' a little money, an' I heard about this pirate, Captain Kidd. Always did want to dig up some buried treasure. Then I had a piece o' luck. I run across a little dried-up professor feller that had found a real old map. He knew it was more'n two hundred years old but didn't have the sense to figger what it meant. I got it for peanuts—only ten thousand bucks—an' I reckon the treasure in this hole here's worth a million, easy. How about splittin' it, fifty-fifty?"

Cramer shook his head. "Sorry, Mr. Roberts," he said, "but there's no treasure buried 'round here. That professor took you good. He's been peddlin' those fake maps to other suckers, an' he must have planted the bones an' the money himself. Go ahead an' dig if you want, but first just remember you'll have to shovel back all the sand when you're through."

The Oklahoman looked at the blisters on his hands and broke into a chuckle. "Nope," he said. "I ain't done this much work in years. Reckon I'm lucky the guy didn't sell me the Brooklyn Bridge! Only one thing—if you have to arrest me, I hope it don't get in the papers. I'd hate to have the boys at the Million-Barrel Club in Tulsa know about this."

"Maybe that can be arranged," Cramer told him with a nod. "Just leave the backbone where it is. Soon as you've filled up the hole again, I'm going to let you get in your boat an' leave. Next time you want to visit Topsail Island, come in through the gate. You'll be shown every courtesy.

By the way, we're looking for your little professor friend. Mind telling us what name he went by?"

"Not a bit," said Roberts. "Like to see him caught. He was introduced to me by a gamblin' chap called Blake. The professor had red hair an' wore thick glasses. His name was Fellenbaum—Dr. Kaspar Fellenbaum."

Don hadn't spoken until now. "Did he spell his first name with a 'K'?" he suddenly asked.

The oilman stared at him. "Why, yes, he did," he replied. "Does that mean anything?"

"It might," said Don. "It was just a hunch I had."

EIGHTEEN

When John Douglas came home that evening and heard all that had happened, he complimented Don on using his head.

"You couldn't have called in a better man than Matt Cramer," he said. "If there'd been any shooting, he'd have taken care of himself and you. Anyhow, he was right to let this Mr. Roberts go. He didn't do any real damage except to his own pride, and his description of the professor sure fits your nasty little friend Fallon. Wonder what his real name is?"

"I'd like to know, too," Don answered. "But whatever it is, I bet we find his initials are K. F. if we catch up with him. We're pretty sure he called himself Kurt Falkenhein and Kaspar Fellenbaum. And if Fallon is his real name, he was probably christened something like Kenneth. Do you think the State Police are going to catch him?"

"They will if he's foolish enough to come back to New Jersey. And I'm pretty sure the New York cops are looking for him, too."

Don wrote a letter to Alec Cameron that night. He remembered his friend had foreseen something like the wealthy oilman's appearance on the scene and would be interested in the day's happenings. Most of all he was sure the biologist would like to know about Mr. Roberts's description of "Dr. Fellenbaum."

"I guess," he wrote, "the thick glasses were just another disguise, but I wonder why he didn't dye his hair or wear a wig. I'm as sure as anything that he's the kidnaper and also the man who is supposed to have found the letter to Captain Kidd's lady friend. He sure knows how to forge old maps, though. They'd fool me quick enough. We've saved the different bones that have been dug up, and they're parts of the school's skeleton, all right. The backbone was all wired together like a string of beads, only Mr. Roberts was too excited to notice. I think he was pretty sore when he found the map was a fake, but he laughed it off. It was different with Varano. He looked as if he wanted to murder somebody."

After he had put the letter in the rural delivery box, Don came back to his room to check again on the bird census. It was impressive enough now to make him proud of his achievement. The idea came to him that he might make pen-and-ink sketches of some of the birds and trace them on a mimeograph stencil. That would make the list even more attractive, he thought.

That evening he suggested the plan to his father, showing him a drawing he had made of a snowy egret.

"Maybe you've got something, Don," said John Douglas after a moment's thought. "Only instead of mimeographing, it would look a lot better if we had the list printed up in a regular pamphlet. Then we could do real justice to your sketches. I have to go to Trenton tomorrow, and if you'll let me take a copy of the list and this drawing, I think I can convince the State Department of Conservation."

His words fired Don's ambition. He hurried back to his room and spent the rest of the evening preparing to draw birds. First he selected a dozen that were interesting and would be easy to draw. For beach birds, he picked the herring gull, laughing gull, common tern, willet, sanderling, and ringed plover. Choosing birds found on the marsh was harder. Certainly he would have to put in one of the white egrets and the great blue heron. He also thought the glossy ibis should be shown, even though it was rather rare. And the osprey because it was so typical of the Jersey coast.

It was when he came to the ducks and geese that he ran into trouble. There were so many of them! He wanted, above all, to include the Canada goose. The snow goose would probably have to be left out, along with the whistling swan. But he felt he must show a mallard and perhaps a pintail or bufflehead duck. In the end, he decided he should make fifteen drawings and leave it to the Director of Conservation to choose.

He could hardly wait for morning to come and was out of bed before his mother started breakfast. All that day he worked on his pencil sketches, checking the drawings against the illustrations in the bird book. Because he took pride in his own skill, he refused to trace the pictures, but he did want his work to be accurate.

By the time his father returned from Trenton that night, Don had finished fifteen birds in pencil.

"Good work!" John Douglas exclaimed with approval. "I sold the director the idea of a printed pamphlet, and he liked your picture of the egret. There isn't much money in the budget for this sort of thing, but if we keep it to twelve pages and use inexpensive line cuts, he thinks we'll get by. Both of us wish we could print it in color, but of course that would cost a lot too much. Anyhow, you go ahead and ink in your drawings. He's eager to see more of 'em."

That was all the encouragement Don needed. The next day was Friday—the end of his vacation week—and he spent all of it at his table, carefully finishing the drawings with a pen and India ink. When at last he spread them all out for his parents to see, he was tired but immensely proud of his accomplishment.

*   *   *

March ended and April came in, warm and pleasant. At school the air was full of baseballs as the boys played catch or batted out flies. Along the sandy stretch of Topsail Island, thousands of migrating birds thronged the beach and the marsh, pausing for a rest and a bite to eat on their long flight northward.

As yet, the only human visitors to the island were a few surf fishermen and an occasional group of bird watchers. Don could identify these people easily, for nearly every one of them carried field glasses or a camera or both. They also brought picnic baskets and ate their lunch on the sand or in the dunes. According to State Park regulations, this was allowed only in a restricted area above the Coast Guard station.

Sometimes Don's father had to drive down the island to warn those who broke the rules, and one weekend he took his son with him. They found half a dozen men and women sitting at the edge of the dune just below the road, eating sandwiches and discussing the birds they had seen. They were all middle-aged or elderly and looked as little like lawbreakers as one could imagine. While John Douglas politely explained to them that they had chosen the wrong spot for a picnic, Don strolled off a few paces, embarrassed at having to listen.

He was standing there on the beach when he noticed a pair of gray-backed sandpipers, a trifle smaller than the numerous sanderlings. It was when they turned at the edge of a wave to run shoreward again that he caught a glimpse of their breasts. The white feathers appeared to be polka-dotted with black spots. Could they be spotted sandpipers? In his excitement he asked the question aloud and was startled to hear it answered.

"Yes," said a woman's voice at his elbow. "Those are spotted sandpipers, and the first I've seen today. You must be interested in birds."

"I live here," he explained, "and I'm trying to make a

census of all the beach and marsh birds I can spot. This one makes fifty-five, counting both fall and spring."

The lady was tall and angular and gray-haired, but she had a pleasant smile. "You've done well!" she complimented him. "All of us watchers together have tallied fewer than forty for the day so far. Of course, I imagine you saw a lot of different ducks during the fall."

"Yes'm, I guess that's what gave me a bigger list. Ducks an' geese an' swans don't stop off here in the spring."

"Well," she said, "I'll have to move on with the others. But when I come back again, I'd like to see the list you've made."

"We're getting it printed," he replied. "I'll mail you one if you'd like."

She sounded genuinely grateful as she gave him her address. "Miss Emily Fothergill's my name," she said. "You can reach me at the Plainfield Library. And don't forget our spotted sandpiper!"

As he rode home with his father, Don told him of the incident. "That's one of the things I like about bird watching," he said. "You meet nice folks, even if they don't always understand rules."

"You're right," John Douglas agreed. "They're fine people. A bit nearsighted sometimes when it comes to reading posted notices, but I like 'em just the same."

At home Don looked up the spotted sandpiper in his book and added the name to his list. Now that he had finished the drawings, he knew he must get the written material in shape for the printer. First he divided the names into two groups —beach birds and marsh birds. Then in each category, he wrote down the common names and arranged them alphabetically. His final task was to do a neat typing job, adding the scientific name for each bird.

That required a careful check on the spelling, and it was late in the evening before he had finished at the typewriter. When he brought the four pages of manuscript to his father, the superintendent's delighted grin was all the praise he needed.

"We'll let the folks at Conservation headquarters decide what the title should be," John Douglas commented. "Remember, though, this is just one boy's list, so don't feel bad if they add a few more names. The night herons, for instance, and probably some others that bird watchers have sighted here. What I expect they'll do is check with the Audubon Society and get their opinion. But I'm proud of the job you've done, Don. When it's printed, with your pic-tures in it, we'll have a mighty interesting pamphlet to hand out."

Two days later the superintendent took the material to Trenton, and Don was waiting anxiously when he came back.

"What happened, Dad?" he asked. "Did they think the stuff was all right?"

"Sure—they're delighted with it. If all goes well, they'll have it printed before the crowds start coming here the end of May. The director sent you his personal congratulations. That isn't all the news, though. I stopped at the State Police barracks for a word with Lieutenant Akins, and he thinks they may be on the trail of Fallon and Blake.

"Last week the New York police located the rooming house where they've been staying and found they'd just packed up and left. Some burned papers in the fireplace looked as if they'd been trying to destroy evidence, and when the police laboratory examined 'em, they found one had been a map, just like the ones we've seen.

"The way it appears now, the two men are heading south. That Cadillac was spotted by a patrol car on the New Jersey Turnpike, not far from the Lincoln Tunnel, yesterday. When it went by, the officers were parked, ticketing a speeder, so it was two or three minutes before they could take off after it. Meanwhile, the Cadillac must have left the pike at the next exit. The patrolman who first noticed the license number said there were two men and a lot of luggage in the car. Akins tells me they've alerted the police in Pennsylvania, Delaware, and Maryland, as well as Jersey."

"Gee!" said Don. "I sure hope they catch 'em before they sell any more maps!"

"That's right. But Akins is more interested in slapping a

kidnaping charge on 'em. If they're caught, you'll probably be called as a witness."

Don hadn't really thought about that. He didn't relish the idea, but he knew it was his duty as a citizen, and he would go through with it if necessary.

As it turned out, he didn't have long to wait. That same evening there was a phone call from Lieutenant Akins, and when his father answered, Don stood close enough to hear all the conversation.

"We've got that pair of con artists," the policeman said. "At least, we're fairly certain these are the men. The big fellow gave his name as Bailey, and the other one with the red hair says he's a Mr. Kelly Feldman. All their papers are in order, of course—probably forged. We'll need you and your son to make a positive identification. Can you come to Tom's River courthouse tomorrow at 10 A.M.?"

"I guess so," John Douglas replied. "The boy's supposed to be in school, of course, but we can stop on the way and explain why he'll be absent."

"Good! See you both in the morning."

Don was much too excited to sleep, and it was well past midnight before he dropped off. When morning came, he had to be wakened by his father.

"Come on, son," the superintendent urged. "We've got to be on the road in less than an hour. Get dressed right away."

At breakfast his mother was worried. "You take care of him, now, John," Don heard her say. "Those men might be dangerous."

"Yes, dear," his father assured her. "I'll see to it he doesn't get hurt."

He was still chuckling when they got into the car and started north.

NINETEEN

After a few minutes spent with the school principal, John Douglas returned to the car, and they set off for Tom's River, a few miles up the road. They reached the courthouse well ahead of the appointed time and found Lieutenant Akins waiting for them in the lobby.

"This shouldn't take too long," he told them. "There'll be a couple of cases ahead of ours, but they're simple enough —drunk and disorderly—driving without a license—that sort of thing. Our friends have got themselves a lawyer, so you may be asked a few questions. Just stick to the truth, and don't let him mix you up."

The hearing was held in a small, dingy courtroom where only a few bored spectators were sitting. The committing magistrate was a shrewd-faced man, past middle age. He looked more like a farmer than a judge, but he knew his law and handled the first two cases with dispatch. When the seedy-looking culprits had been sent off to do time in the county workhouse, the bailiff rose and spoke in a rapid singsong.

"State versus Bailey and Feldman," he intoned. "The accused will rise an' face the bench."

There they were—the hulking figure of Blake and the smaller redhead. Don stole a look at their backs. When they were seated again, the county attorney addressed the court.

"This is a fairly serious case, Your Honor," he announced. "I shall ask that these defendants be held for the grand jury on two charges—felonious assault with intent to do bodily harm—and kidnaping."

At that last word, the audience sat up in surprise, and two or three reporters hastily grabbed for paper and pencils. The prosecutor briefly outlined the events of Friday, the twenty-seventh of March, then called Don as his first witness.

After giving his name, age, and address, the boy was allowed to tell his own story. He tried to make it factual, without any frills, but when he came to the part about being left, bound and blindfolded, in the isolated shack, there were some shocked faces among the spectators.

"What time of day was it when they left you?" asked the prosecutor.

"Around six or six-thirty," Don replied. "I know it was getting dark when I got the blindfold off."

"And about what was the temperature?"

"I don't know exactly, but it had been chilly all day, with a north wind. It sure felt cold there in the shack."

"Now," said the attorney, "about this blow on the back of your head—did you see a doctor after you were rescued?"

"No, sir. All I had in the morning was a swelled place and a headache. It got better after a while. I didn't make any fuss about it because I didn't want to scare my mother."

There was a murmur of sympathy at this, and the judge called sternly for order.

"Before you were blindfolded," the prosecutor went on, "did you get a good look at the men who carried you off in the boat?"

"Yes, sir."

"And is either of them here in this courtroom?"

For the first time, Don allowed himself to stare at the

prisoners. Some effort had been made to change their appearance, but he recognized them easily enough. The big dark one had had his hair closely cropped, and the other man was wearing glasses and a luxuriant auburn mustache. However, the sharp-nosed, foxy face was the same.

"There they are, both of them," said Don firmly, and pointed at the pair.

The defense lawyer jumped to his feet, but the judge silenced him. "You'll have your chance in cross-examination," he said crisply. "Has the prosecution finished with this witness?"

"Yes, Your Honor. I may want to recall him later, but we're ready for the defense to cross-examine."

Don drew a deep breath to steady himself as the opposing attorney stepped forward belligerently. "You say," he addressed Don with a sneer, "you walked all the way from your home to the place where this alleged assault took place. About eight miles I believe you called it. Isn't that quite a walk for a cripple?"

Don's face flushed. "It's the best exercise I can take," he answered. "If I could do it every day, my leg would soon be well."

"Now," the lawyer went on, "what makes you so sure these men had anything to do with it? As a matter of fact, have you ever set eyes on them before today?"

"Yes," said Don. "Several times. They called themselves by different names—Blake and Fallon—and they've tried to change their looks, too. But it was that big one who hit me on the head, and the smaller one gave the orders. That phoney mustache wouldn't fool anyone for a minute. Let me pull it, and I bet it'll come off."

Again the judge frowned and rapped for order while laughter sounded through the room.

"Bailiff," he said, "I think you should try what the witness suggests."

There was a howl of protest from the defense attorney, but the husky court attendant followed orders. A moment later the big red mustache lay in the palm of his hand.

When the uproar died down, the judge gave the defense lawyer a pitying look. "Do you want to call any witnesses?" he asked. "If not, the court feels this case has gone far enough. I hereby order the defendants held for the grand jury, and in view of the severity of the case, bail for each is set at twenty-five thousand dollars."

Don stepped down from the witness box in a daze. An instant later, his father had an arm around him and Lieutenant Akins was shaking his hand. Then Alec Cameron joined them. Don hadn't seen him in the courtroom, but he was there, ready to testify if needed. After that it was the prosecutor's turn to congratulate him.

"That was a stroke of genius, boy." He grinned. "Easiest case I ever won. We'll make it stick all the way to a conviction, too. Of course, New York wants them on a fraud charge, and all in all they're in trouble up to their necks."

"Think they'll be able to raise that much bail?" John Douglas asked.

"It's hard to say," Lieutenant Akins replied. "But they'll have a tough time skipping the country if they do. We'll watch 'em like a hawk."

"I'm sure you will," Alec Cameron put in. "But I'd hate to be in their shoes if—well, never mind. Just keep an eye on them and hope they stay alive."

The police officer raised his eyebrows, then nodded. "I see what you mean," he said soberly. "Will do—and I'll tip off the men in New York, in case they head back there again."

"One other thing," the biologist added. "There was certainly some hook-up between the kidnapers and that fellow who rents boats—what's his name—Jimson. Their car was seen there several times, and Don says it was one of Jimson's outboards they had that night. It might be a good idea to question Mr. Jimson and that son of his. The bones buried down the island were definitely parts of a skeleton taken from Ocean Regional High School."

Akins made a note of the names. "I'll do that," he agreed. "It ought to strengthen our case."

* * *

At school the next day, Don found himself something of a celebrity. It was the first time any word of his kidnaping had been made public, and many of the youngsters gathered around to ask respectful questions about his experience. There was one exception. Digger Jimson stayed as far away as he could, and even in the bus that afternoon he kept strangely silent, his nose buried in a history book.

After he got home, Don was restless. With his bird project finished and turned over to the state, he felt at loose ends. Perhaps what he needed was exercise, he thought. So he called Bullet and started hiking down the beach.

He had gone only a little over a mile when the pick-up truck stopped on the road above him, and his father hailed him. To Don's surprise the teacher, Garry Reynolds, was with him in the cab.

"We're going down the island to do a little digging," John Douglas said. "Want to come along?"

In a moment Don and the dog were in the back of the truck and headed south. His father stopped near the blazed cedar, where they took their shovels and crossed the dune.

"I'd like to see how many bones I can get back," Reynolds said with a grin.

Each of the three picked a separate spot to dig, and soon

the sand was flying. Even Bullet had caught the contagion. He sniffed around till he found a likely place and dug his own hole, almost as fast as the shovelers.

It was the teacher who made the first find. With a yell he held up the lower jaw of a skull and a moment later discovered the rest of the round bleached head, deeper in the sand. Don was working where the Oklahoma oilman had dug, and though the spinal column had been taken away, he found two Spanish pieces of eight about four feet down.

Then Bullet came up with a long thigh bone gripped in his teeth, and before long the superintendent discovered the bones of a lower leg from kneecap to toes. They kept on toiling for another hour without finding any additional parts of the skeleton.

"That's queer," said Reynolds, mopping his brow. "There ought to be more here—the ribs and shoulder bones and arms, another whole leg, and the pelvis."

"Maybe they didn't bury any more," Don suggested. "Just enough to use as bait for the suckers who bought the maps. The rest of the skeleton's probably a long way from here."

They took the bones they had and returned to the head of the island, where Reynolds had left his car. It wasn't until Don had gone to bed that an idea came to him. He remembered Bill Newton's story of seeing Digger Jimson late one night, carrying a lantern and a shovel. Was that what the boy had been doing—burying the unused parts of the skeleton? If so, they were probably under the sand in the backyard of the bait store, somewhere between the house and the dock.

He mentioned the idea to his father at breakfast, but John Douglas was inclined to smile at his hunches.

"I doubt if there's anything to it," he said, "but I'll speak to Lieutenant Akins the next time I'm in touch with him. After all, the Jimsons are neighbors, of a sort. We don't want to get them into more trouble than they're already in."

Reluctantly Don dropped the subject, and as the weeks of early spring went by, he almost forgot about it. The pace of schoolwork quickened, with the end of the term drawing nearer, but Don still found time to hike along the beach or explore the bay shore of the island in the boat.

By the third week in April, many of the marsh waders had returned and could be seen feeding along the creek banks. It was one evening about seven, just before sunset, that he saw a black-crowned night heron leave its treetop roost and fly westward toward the mudflats. It was about the size of a large crow, but its gray back, black cap, and white breast made it easy to distinguish from other birds. Only its night-feeding habits made it so hard to find. Don waited till it landed on the marsh so that he could get a view of the length of the legs. Then he was certain he could add another bird to his list. His father had told him he would have a chance to read the printer's proofs, and the night heron's name could be inserted at that time.

When he got home and tied up the boat, it was beginning to grow dark, but there was still light enough to see the black-and-white police car in the dooryard. He entered the house and found Lieutenant Akins talking to his father in the living room.

"Luckily," the officer was saying, "the New York force had two good detectives tailing them. They weren't close enough to stop the shooting, but they did catch Varano. He'd pulled up to the curb in a closed car and fired three or four bursts from a machine gun. The little fellow, Fallon, was killed instantly. Blake caught half a dozen slugs through the belly, but he was still alive when he reached the hospital. Before he died, he gave the detectives a confession that covered the treasure hoax—the kidnaping—just about everything."

Akins saw Don standing in the doorway and turned to him. "Well, son," he said, "I guess this means you won't have to testify before the grand jury after all. The gunman, Varano, was caught dead to rights, and he'll go up for life. There were a dozen witnesses to the killing."

Don couldn't help shivering. He remembered the look on Varano's face when they told him the treasure map was a fake. The gangster had been taken for a sucker, and murder was the only answer under his code.

"By the way, Lieutenant," John Douglas remarked. "I've been meaning to tell you about an idea Don had. Seems another lad saw young Dick Jimson late one night with a lantern and a shovel. He was coming up from the direction of the dock, back of their boat rental place. As you know, the two con men were operating from Jimsons' and using their boats. This is a small matter," he went on apologetically, "but Don wondered if maybe Dick was burying part of the skeleton that was stolen from the school."

"Hm," said Akins, frowning. "I've wanted to talk to the Jimsons anyway. I'll see what we can find out."

Don was pretty quiet after the policeman had gone. He had been shocked by the news of Varano's double killing, but more than that, his conscience troubled him. Was there really any proof that Digger Jimson had stolen the skeleton? Or was he himself trying to get back at the other boy for some of his taunts? He began to hope that Akins would find no serious connection between the Jimsons and the two men who were now dead.

Early the following week, Don got aboard the school bus one morning and was surprised to see that Digger wasn't in his usual seat.

"Where's our friend?" he asked Bill Newton jokingly.

"I dunno—Tom's River, maybe. All I heard was that a

State Police car stopped there this morning, an' Digger an' his father got in. You reckon the cops have arrested 'em?"

"Gee," said Don, "I hope not! Now that Blake an' Fallon are gone, I thought the whole case was finished. Maybe they just want to ask 'em some questions."

The next day young Jimson was back in school, much to Don's relief. He seemed to be a lot less cocky than usual, however, and kept largely to himself. After school that afternoon, Don saw him with a mop and pail, cleaning up the biology laboratory, while Garry Reynolds put away the microscopes and other equipment.

It was two days later that he found out the cause of this activity. John Douglas came home and reported having talked to the police lieutenant.

"I guess they gave the Jimsons a pretty stiff grilling," he said. "Dick's father seems to be in the clear, even though he might have suspected something fishy was going on. But it was different with the boy. He admits he got twenty-five dollars for blazing that cedar and staining the cut to make it look old. And then when they told him they wanted some human bones, he stole a set of keys, went back to school with them in the Cadillac at night, and got the skeleton out of the closet. Fallon gave him another fifty dollars for that. And you were right, Don, about his burying what was left of the skeleton in the back yard.

"Apparently the judge decided Dick got sort of carried away by the idea of helping to find Captain Kidd's treasure and probably really believed it was here on the island. Since he's just a kid, they put him on probation, but he has to work out the cost of the skeleton by helping around the laboratory after school."

"Gosh," Don said in relief, "I'm glad it turned out that way. I was afraid they might put him in reform school."

TWENTY

The last six weeks of school before summer vacation had always seemed to pass slowly, but this spring Don was too busy to think about it. The proofs of the bird census came from the printer early in May, and he read and reread them to make sure there were no errors.

As he expected, the State Conservation Department had added the names of a number of birds occasionally seen on Topsail Island. Among them were the yellow-crowned night heron, king rail, royal tern, hooded merganser, avocet, and horned grebe. He was familiar with the pictures and descriptions of all of them from his *Water Bird Guide*, and with any luck, he hoped to spot and identify them himself before the season ended. The grand total now came to sixty-two—enough, Don thought, to whet the appetites of bird watchers all over the East.

What made him proudest of all were the little line engravings of birds made from his pen-and-ink drawings. Reduced in size, they looked so clean and sharp, he could hardly believe they were his own.

The title of the pamphlet was to be "Beach and Marsh Birds of Topsail Island," and if all went well, it would be ready for distribution before Memorial Day. That was the time when the first big influx of visitors might be expected.

A week later came a wedding invitation. Miss Amanda

Carter and Dr. Alexander Cameron were to be married in Maine on the eighteenth of June.

With the event only a month away, Don began to worry about what he could give them for a wedding present. It was his mother who gave him the answer.

"Those line drawings you did," she said, "are so nice in

black and white that I wish you'd make bigger ones and paint them with water color. Don't you think the bride and groom would love to have such pictures? They were both so interested in your bird watching."

Happy with the idea, Don set to work that very evening. On larger paper he made four sketches—a mallard drake, a black skimmer, a great black-backed gull, and a glossy ibis. They were chosen because each one gave him an opportunity to use bold, bright color. The painting was more difficult, but after a week of hard work, he was finally satisfied with the finished pictures.

Now that he knew he could do it well, he made a secret resolve to paint more birds. He could put them up around his room. Perhaps, he dared to think, he might even find a market for such pictures at the souvenir stores on the upper island!

*   *   *

Everyone at school agreed that Miss Carter had never looked prettier than in those final weeks before the term ended. She was so happy and so engrossed in her coming marriage that it might have been hard for her to enforce discipline in class. However, none of the students took advantage of the fact.

On the third Saturday in May, Don's father reminded him that they had an appointment with the doctor in Philadelphia. It was time for the yearly check-up he had always dreaded. The two of them drove through the New Jersey pinelands, then through peach and apple orchards pink with bloom. They passed new suburban developments, then crossed one of the big bridges over the Delaware River, and finally entered the city.

When they reached the clinic, there was a long wait. Don's spirits sank as he sat there and watched the other patients—nearly all young people like himself. Some wore braces or walked with difficulty. Some swung along on crutches. A few were even in wheel chairs. It gave him a sharp twinge of pity to see these boys and girls limp into the doctor's office, and he offered a silent prayer of thanks that he no longer suffered as they did.

When his turn came, the physician greeted him with a grin.

"You're looking pretty fit, my boy," he said. "Let's see you walk across the room. Good! Now try a knee-bend, slow and easy. Does that hurt? Hardly at all, eh? All right, let me check your reflexes."

The doctor took notes on each of a series of tests. Finally he stood up and held out his hand.

"Whatever you've been doing, Don," he commented, "it's evidently the right treatment. Lots of hiking on the beach, I expect, and swimming, too. I wish all my patients could get the same kind of exercise. You're almost back to normal now, and if you keep it up, you won't need any help from me. By this time next year, I predict you'll be walking and running as well as anybody."

"You mean," Don said slowly, "I won't have to come back here any more?"

"Not unless you run into trouble of some kind, and I don't think there's much chance of that."

John Douglas was as pleased as his son. They left the clinic and walked a few blocks to a famous confectionery store, where they enjoyed the biggest and richest chocolate malteds Don had ever tasted. Then, full almost to bursting, they started the drive home.

"Five years ago," said Don's father, "it was all you could do to get from one room to another. Your mother and I were pretty discouraged—afraid you'd never have a full, active life like other kids. Now look at you! And most of the credit belongs to you. Even when it hurt, you wouldn't give up. I'm proud of you, son!"

* * *

During the last week in May, a big package from Trenton was delivered at the superintendent's house. In it were three thousand copies of Don's bird pamphlet. A letter from the Conservation Commissioner also arrived. A thousand more copies, he wrote, had been sent to Audubon Society headquarters, and he expected that many bird watchers would be visiting Topsail Island as a result.

Don looked forward eagerly to the long Memorial Day weekend. But when he rose on Saturday morning, it was raining, and the wind was out of the east. That, he thought, meant practically nobody would visit the island.

His father called the gate before sitting down to breakfast, and when he came back to the table, his face wore a look of surprise.

"I wouldn't have believed it," he said, "but two busloads of Audubon Society people just pulled in. A few fishermen have come down, too. Maybe we'll have a good enough crowd after all."

As soon as he had eaten, Don hurried off to the gatehouse. The rain grew lighter and stopped entirely by ten o'clock, and more cars kept arriving. As each party signed the register, Don passed out the mimeographed sheets listing the island's trees and plants, then offered his own bird pamphlet. He was pleased to find how many people had been attracted to Topsail to look for sea birds. On this day, at least, they far outnumbered the fishermen.

Cramer, on duty at the gate, watched suspiciously for any would-be treasure hunters. After the killing of Fallon and Blake, there had been a lot of publicity, with the whole subject of Captain Kidd's treasure raked over once more in the tabloids. However, nearly all the visitors were carrying field glasses or cameras—a fairly sure test of an interest in birds rather than treasure.

Just before noon, Don left for home. There had been no new arrivals for the past half hour, and it looked as if the stream of tourists was about over. Then, as he walked down the road, he heard a horn honk behind him. Even before he turned, he knew the sound came from Alec Cameron's Volkswagen. The little car pulled up alongside, and there was the happy couple smiling at him.

"Get in!" cried Alec. "We'll drive you home in state!"

It seemed they had phoned ahead in Don's absence and were invited to lunch. That was a gay meal—one of the best Don ever remembered. Both Amanda and Alec were full of their plans for a home in Princeton and, if possible, a small summer cottage as near Topsail Island as they could get.

"We want to be able to keep an eye on this sprout here." Alec chuckled. "Amanda hopes he'll be a bird artist, and I want to make a good solid scientist out of him. If he turns out to be both, so much the better. Donny, that pamphlet of yours is a fine piece of work."

"Thanks," said Don, reddening with pleasure. "But I guess you know you had a lot to do with it. Look at all the birds you spotted that I'd missed."

"I didn't teach you to draw, though," the professor answered with a grin. "Those pictures are so real, I'd recognize the birds anywhere."

Don rose from the table. "Maybe this is the right time," he said, "for me to show you your wedding present. It isn't wrapped up fancy, and it didn't cost much, but it shows what I think of you both."

He raced upstairs and gathered his bird paintings together.

Before he came down, he found a piece of blue ribbon on the table in his mother's room, rolled the paintings up, and tied a neat bow around them.

"Here," he said in embarrassment, handing the roll to Amanda Carter. "It's for the two of you."

Soberly she untied the ribbon and spread the pictures out.

"Ooh!" she said, catching her breath. "Don, they're simply beautiful! Didn't I tell you, Alec, he was born to be an artist?"

"So you did," he replied. "But please notice that every detail is accurate. That's the mark of your true scientist! All kidding aside, Don, these are wonderful. I'll let my bride decide where to hang them, but you can bet they'll be decorating our new home!"

He stood up and raised his glass of iced tea. "To the pirate treasure that wasn't there!" he said. "And to the things Don Douglas found instead!"

www.ingramcontent.com/pod-product-compliance
Lightning Source LLC
Chambersburg PA
CBHW060601190726
48283CB00003B/1103